T0120832

RESTORING FOR
LOVE

A Christian Romance

JUDITH ANNE STAPLES

WESTBOW
P R E S S®
A DIVISION OF THOMAS NELSON
& ZONDERVAN

WestBow Press books may be ordered through booksellers or by contacting:

WestBow Press
A Division of Thomas Nelson & Zondervan
1663 Liberty Drive
Bloomington, IN 47403
www.westbowpress.com
844-714-3454

Scripture quotations marked (CEV) are from the Contemporary English Version Copyright © 1991, 1992, 1995 by American Bible Society. Used by Permission.

ISBN: 978-1-6642-4689-8 (sc)
ISBN: 978-1-6642-4688-1 (e)

Print information available on the last page.

WestBow Press rev. date: 10/06/2021

"You, Lord, brought me safely through birth, and you protected me when I was a baby at my mother's breast. From the day I was born, I have been in your care, and from the time of my birth you have been my God."

Psalm 22:9-10
(*The Holy Bible, Contemporary English Version*)

ONE

It was one of those refreshing spring days that made Peyton Carmichael happy to enjoy a trip in northern Alberta. The sky was blue with cotton-ball clouds here and there, and the air was spiked with the first real warmth of the season. Aspen and larch trees lining the highway were starting to bud, and the adjoining pastures were dotted with cattle and horses enjoying the first sprouts. With her motorhome window rolled partway down, and her favorite music playing, she had to resist the urge to speed. She loved the outdoors and was excited for the opportunity to head to a new adventure, away from the noise and crowds of the big city where she had grown up, and into the beautiful Rocky Mountains.

Peyton's destination was Rocky View, a small town in the foothills of the mountains, several hundred miles from the city she called home. A month before, she and her father Dave had purchased a rural property there, with help from her aunt Julie, a realtor who lived in the nearby community. Dave and Peyton were experienced house flippers who had renovated several urban homes over the years, and when an interesting property came up for sale, Julie immediately thought of her brother-in-law and niece. It would be a perfect project for them, and she would love to have them come and spend time with her and her husband Ed, to help restore neglected the Mountain View Lodge, near a National Park.

When Julie first contacted them with the opportunity, Dave had been reluctant to consider it. He thought it was too far away from their home, and too big an undertaking. It would be more than just a renovation. They would have to purchase the Lodge, restore it and then sell it again for a profit. Dave protested that it would cost too much, although that wouldn't be a problem. Their company, Carmichael Constructions, had a reputation for doing beautiful renewal projects, and they had substantial funds and the ability to do an excellent job. Peyton was excited right off the bat, and when they finally coached her dad to consider it, spent hours talking with Julie on the phone and analyzing the photos she sent to them. Dave was finally persuaded to at least visit the site, and a friend offered to fly them to the town. After examining the Lodge and visiting the charming little town nearby, they all agreed it would be a great opportunity to restore the hotel that had been in business years ago.

The proximity to the National Park would surely attract tourists year-round. Accommodations inside the Park were expensive, and many vacationers preferred to remain outside and just do day trips. Mountain View Lodge had a history of boarding people in the past. Admittedly it was in poor condition and needed a makeover to higher standards, but once the renovations were completed, it would make an excellent Bed and Breakfast and more.

The Lodge had been vacant for the last five years, and for sale the last eight months. The owner lived in another country and was tired of paying a caretaker to look after the property. Dave told Julie to go ahead and make an offer, and with her realtor expertise she was able to negotiate for an amazingly low price and it was accepted! Dave and Peyton were delighted, and within a couple of weeks, their purchase was complete.

Now, a month later, Peyton was driving to the mountains she loved, on her way to beginning the project. Dave had estimated that it would take about three months to complete the job, so they were taking their motorhome to stay in on site. Peyton had loaded their personal belongings inside, and Dave packed the storage area underneath with tools and equipment they would need. He had recently had the motorhome inspected, and the pickup truck double-checked, since they would be driving a such a long distance. When they were finally ready to go, he wanted to travel with her, but at the last moment decided to stop at the bank and get some cash. Peyton persuaded him to let her go ahead. The motorhome would be slower, so he would catch up with her anyway.

Peyton had not been on a trip to the mountains for years and was thrilled with the opportunity. She was an only child and her mother was a city girl who hated camping, so when she was young, her grandparents took her with them camping every summer in the Rockies. Dave liked the outdoors too but couldn't leave his busy construction business in the summer, so it became a tradition for other family members to take Peyton with them on the holidays. She loved it! T Since then, both her mother Melissa and the grandparents had passed away, and other family members lived in different areas of Canada, so they rarely met. Peyton's summers consisted of working with her dad, and they rarely took holidays. This mountain adventure was going to be a treat for them both.

Carmichael Construction started out as a small business but had come a long way. For over thirty years, Dave had been a successful new-homes contractor and had never thought of doing anything else. Then one day a fellow worker approached him and asked if he would be interested in doing a house flip. At the time, Peyton was in in her final year of high school, with plans to become a journeyman carpenter. She had taken required courses in math, drafting and carpentry, and she was helping her dad with projects whenever she could. Doing a house flip seemed like a good opportunity for Peyton to go further so they accepted the challenge. Giving that first home a renewal was very satisfying and enabled Peyton to complete the apprenticeship courses with her dad as her sponsor. Now she was a Journeyman Carpenter with several years of experience. They had done many flips together, all in the big city though. This would be their first rural job.

Strangely, Peyton didn't see Dave as they travelled. Surely, he would have caught up with her long ago. She had made several stops on the way, each time waiting a few minutes for him. Perhaps he had passed her when she was inside a washroom or gas station, but he would have noticed the motorhome. She tried to get him on his phone, but it kept going to Voicemail. Maybe he had forgotten his charger…something he frequently did and was scolded for. She felt uneasy but kept driving herself, hoping he didn't have trouble with his truck. She had hoped to get to the site before nightfall but it didn't happen. Dusk fell and when she finally arrived at the Lodge, she was surprised to see that he was not there.

Aunt Julie was waiting for her with open arms. "I'm so glad to see you, honey. What a long trip! You must be tired. I'm surprised to see you driving this big rig. Where's your dad?"

Peyton avoided telling her aunt that Dave might have a problem. "He should be here soon. We planned to travel together but I wanted to get a head start." She took a deep breath of the crisp mountain air and gazed around. "It's great to see you, Auntie! I'm so happy to be here. This is going to be a wonderful experience for us."

"I'm really glad you and Dave bought the Lodge, Peyton. I just love it. It's the nicest, most unique place I've ever listed since I started in real estate. I know you will work your magic and make it fantastic." She shook her finger at Peyton. "The only thing that bothers me is that you're not planning to live here yourself. I was hoping you'd like it so much that you'd settle down close to us."

"You know that's not possible, Auntie. We have several people on a list who want us to do house renovations, and even a few business places. We're going to be very busy this summer. But we love the work we do, and I'm hoping there'll be plenty time for us to enjoy some mountain activities too."

"The Lodge is gorgeous, isn't it?" The red brick building was three stories high, with several peaks and pretty dormers, nestled among huge fir trees. "The exterior seems not too bad, in fairly good condition. It's mainly the inside that needs a make-over." Peyton gazed up with a wide smile and shining eyes. "This is going to be awesome. I fell in love with this place the moment we saw it last month. If Dad were here, he would say that I do that with every flip we have done but this one is special."

Just then a horn tooted, and they turned to see a pickup truck drive into the yard. Not Dave's but a long-legged young man hopped out and joined them. "Hello there, ladies…how are you? Hope I'm not interrupting."

"Hello yourself, stranger!" Julie was all smiles as she gave him a hug. "Where have you been lately? We've missed you. Overseas with your logs?"

"Just got back last night from Sweden. Business as usual."

"Good timing, Tom. Come and meet my lovely niece!" Peyton blushed as the man with dark curly hair and a shadow of beard reached out to shake her hand in a firm grip. She found herself looking into the bluest eyes she'd ever seen. "Peyton Carmichael," Julie said, with an impish grin, "this is your new neighbor! Tom lives down the road and builds log homes for people all over the world."

He reached out to clasp her hand. "Tom McCauley. Pleased to meet you, Peyton. Welcome to the neighborhood! Julie told me some folks had purchased the Lodge and were going to restore it. That's wonderful! It is about time it had new owners. Need some help unloading? I'd be happy to help."

"Thanks, but I can manage. We don't have much to do right now, and my father will be here soon." She smiled and linked arms with Julie. "It's so beautiful here! I'm thankful that Aunt Julie found it for us."

Tom smiled. "You'll love living in this area. I've lived here my whole life and every day is a gift to me. It'll be nice for you to be close to family, won't it? Especially these folks. Your aunt and uncle are like family to me."

Peyton opened her mouth to comment that it would just be temporary, but Tom continued. "This is a beautiful neighborhood. My house is not far away, just around the curve on the right, one in a loop of acreages. Great area, but Julie, have you warned her about the grizzly bears and cougars?"

"Oh, stop it." Julie slapped at his arm. "A bear or two, maybe once a year. Nothing to worry about. Mostly just deer and elk. A treat to watch, especially this time of year when the babies come. You'll love it!"

Tom grinned and squeezed her arm. "Just kidding,

Peyton. I'm on my way home from work and had to snoop when I saw your motorhome. This Lodge has not been lived in for years. So glad it will open again. Well, I won't keep you folks. Our church is having a Chili Cook-Off tonight, and these folks have entered. Is Ed bringing his special recipe, Julie?"

"Oh, he's already there. That man! He's been planning for this all week. He thinks he'll be a shoo-in for First Prize."

"Well, he can have my vote," Tom laughed. "I've eaten his chili before and it gets better every year. But I'm not judging this year, so he'll have to convince the others." He turned to Peyton. "Would you like to come along? Everyone is welcome."

"Sounds tempting but no thanks." Peyton smiled. "Dad should be here soon and it's been a long day. I just want to settle in and be here when he arrives."

"Understood. Well, please feel free to call on me if you need help anytime. Just around the curve, a log house with a big blue spruce. Nice to meet you!" With another smile and wave, he jumped in the truck and drove away.

Julie turned back to Peyton with a big grin. "Well, what do you think of Tom? Isn't he nice? I was hoping he'd stop by so you could meet him."

"He does seem very friendly, and it was kind of him to offer his help."

"He's like that. Such a great guy! He would do anything to help others. Everyone in town thinks a lot of him. Ed and I have known him since he was a baby and look at him now!" She chuckled. "The women in our town think he's handsome, including me. We can't understand why he isn't married yet. He is almost thirty and still a bachelor. Just hasn't found the right gal yet, I guess." She lifted her eyebrows and smiled. "You should get to know him better, honey. You're so lovely. Slim and pretty, with your long chestnut curls and that beautiful smile. I could tell Tom was impressed."

"Auntie! Let's not talk about that stuff." Recalling her aunt was always trying to be a matchmaker, Peyton steered the conversation back to the property. "Tell me more about this area. You mentioned before that it's a subdivision. How many acreages are there in the loop? I meant to take a walk through there the last time we were here, but we didn't have the time."

"There are seven all together. Some are bigger, some smaller, and they are all built back from the road for privacy except for this one. All are considered residential except for this one, because it's a hotel. The area is so beautiful! There is a trail that goes to an outlook point with a stellar view. When you get settled in and have some time, I'll take you on a hike. We can see Tom's house on our way. He built it himself and it's awesome! One of the nicest in the loop. Come now, let's go inside. I brought some coffee and groceries for you and turned up the heat a bit. I can't wait to hear about what you and Dave have planned for the renovations."

The Lodge entry way opened into a huge hallway with several doorways - one of which led to the kitchen and dining area, and another to a huge great room. Beautiful hand carved woodwork was everywhere – on the front desk, walls and doors, and the staircase to the other floors. Several pieces of lovely furniture had been left behind in the sale, and Julie had removed the covers in the great room in time for their arrival. Peyton had worked with her dad to make blueprints on her tablet and now she was happy to share it with her aunt. A few clicks, and Peyton showed Julie what they had in mind.

"As you know Auntie, the Lodge was built in the

1950's as a vacation hotel destination. Over the years, other people lived in it as families, but we will advertise it now for tourists. It will be a lovely option for those who want to visit the National Park but don't want to pay for expensive accommodations. We're changing things somewhat to make room for more guests. These kitchen and dining rooms are way too small for the number of guests we're planning to have, so we will expand them and bring in some commercial equipment, new appliances and cupboards, a big island, and a walk-in pantry. We'll make the dining and great rooms open plan."

Julie was admiring the space. "I love it, Peyton. The vaulted ceilings and that huge fireplace are so amazing! And the bay windows are lovely too. I can just picture the guests and their families lounging in here after a long day of fun in the park. Some of these windows need to be either restored or replaced, so that will be a challenge, but worth it for those beautiful views."

"In the city, it's so crowded," Peyton sighed. "Houses are so close together you can practically shake hands with your neighbors out the window. We plan to put sliding doors to the back yard instead of those two French doors and build a new deck and pergola. If we add some nice landscaping and a fire pit of some kind, it will be a lovely place for guests to enjoy the outdoors."

Peyton continued to show her more of the blueprints. It appeared that most of the main floor needed to be restored, as did other parts of the Lodge. Thankfully, some of the oak floors had been sealed in the past, so they would just need a hardwood floor cleaner to spruce them up. The second story plan showed a spacious master bedroom with its large ensuite and walk-in closet. "We will be ripping up a lot of carpets and other flooring in the bedrooms. There might be something underneath that just needs cleaning and polishing. If not, we will replace with them something more contemporary. There are so many beautiful choices now a days. We'll be re-modelling all the bathrooms too."

"Six bedrooms including the master." Julie frowned and looked closer at the tablet. "There are five other bedrooms and only one bathroom for all those guests? That's not very much."

"Yes, I know. We may change the plans to renovate the third-floor loft as well, which right now is just a storage area, and put the master suite up there. We need to examine it and see what we can do. If all goes well, we'll knock down some walls on the second floor and make more bedrooms, with an ensuite in each one. A lot of work but it will be worth it."

Julie excused herself, needing to attend the Cook-Off, and hugged Peyton goodbye, promising to come again soon. Peyton wandered out to the backyard. Just being out there in such a beautiful setting was a pleasure. Looking up into the trees, she took a deep breath of the fragrant mountain air. No noise or smog like the city. Even though a lot of work needed to be done, surely there would be opportunities to spend some time outdoors.

Dave would enjoy it too but where was he? What was taking him so long to get there? He had been as eager to travel as she was. She thought everything had been arranged for the project. Maybe things at home were taking more time than he had planned. Perhaps he had stopped for a meal on the way. Understandable but she felt queasy. The sun was down now and she did not like the idea of him driving in the dark. She found her phone and tried again to call him but he didn't answer, still voicemail. Sighing, she went back to the motorhome and had a snack. She would wait to have a bigger meal with Dave when he arrived.

How she loved this place! While her mind said this was just another flip, her heart was saying it would make a great forever home. She smiled to imagine living there with a big dog for company, to keep those "grizzlies and cougars" away. She would have to get a cat too of course, since country houses always had mouse problems. She knew she was being silly, but this was the first reno, of all the ones they had done in the past, that she felt passionate about. This was a place that she would love to live in herself.

Maybe with a handsome neighbor like Tom McCauley. She blushed, thinking about their meeting. She had been bowled over by those blue eyes and felt a bit tongue-tied. The fact was, she had never been much interested in having a boyfriend, not even in high school, although several guys had tried to date her. She was too busy completing her carpenter apprenticeship and once it was official, working as an employee of Carmichael Construction. Her mother, Melissa was a lawyer, happy with her life and proud of her only daughter, although at times wondering why Peyton had chosen that career. Sadly, a few years after her graduation, Melissa was diagnosed with stage four metastatic cancer. Dave and Peyton stopped working and looked after her until she passed away a few months later. They were both devastated, especially Dave for the loss of his wife. He became depressed and didn't go back to work for several months, depending on Peyton to look after home and business matters. Eventually things got somewhat better, but even though it was several years ago, Peyton missed her mother every day.

Peyton sighed and thought about this flip they were now committed to. She and her dad both loved what they did, but after Melissa died their lives had never been quite the same. The Lodge was like the 80's and it would take a lot of work to make it contemporary. Being so far from their city home increased their expenses but working there would be a breath of fresh air in their lives. When Tom mentioned his church activities, she had felt a pang of envy. Her parents had been devoted Christians for most of their lives and raised Peyton that way, but they had not set a foot into the church since Melissa's funeral. Peyton felt a pang of remorse. Perhaps it was time to re-kindle that flame.

TWO

Later that evening, Peyton made another call to Dave, trying to assure him that she had arrived safely and was looking forward to his arrival. The call still went to voicemail. She sighed and left another message. She had finished unloading equipment and supplies into the Lodge and locked the doors. It was getting dark outside and she was feeling uneasy in the motorhome. Her heart jumped when she heard a loud knock on the door. That had to be her dad now, although she had not heard his truck. Turning on the outside light, she was surprised to see Tom, juggling a crock pot and paper bags.

"Hi, Peyton! Me again!" He flashed his 100watt smile as he struggled through the doorway with the pot. "Julie and Ed asked me bring you some left-overs. Can you grab the bags? I think something's going to fall any minute."

Peyton led the way into the little kitchenette and set the bags on the counter, peeking inside to see milk, cereal, fresh fruits and coffee. "I stopped on the way home and bought a few things for you," Tom said sheepishly. My contribution from the Welcome Brigade."

"Thank you so much, Tom. Have a seat. Looks yummy! This is great." Peyton smiled as she peeked at the chili and inhaled the delicious aroma. "Looks like prize-winning to me. Did Ed win?"

"He did!" Tom laughed. "And he was insufferable, crowing about it to the other contestants. All in fun, of course. The good news is that we raised a nice sum for our Guatemala mission project. And had a great time doing it. Have you eaten?"

"Not really. I had a bite a while ago but lost track of the time. Still waiting for my dad but he hasn't shown up. I'm really worried that he isn't here by now."

"I'm sure he'll be along soon." He rooted around in the bag and pulled out a big spoon, napkins, and plastic soup bowls. "Julie thought of everything. It may not be as warm as you'd like it."

"That's okay. It looks delicious," she smiled as she dug in. "Would you like some? There's still plenty for Dad." She handed him a warm bowl of chili and gestured for him to sit. "We can heat his up if necessary."

"I've had my fill, thanks. If I have anymore, I'll regret it."

"Have you ever been inside the Lodge, Tom?"

"Strangely, no. When we were kids, we thought it was haunted and we didn't want to go near it. As an adult, I didn't really care about it. I bought my property five years ago and the Lodge was still empty then. Apparently, a family lived here years ago, then had to sell it because the county changed the by-law and they couldn't keep their horses here. No large livestock is allowed unless the acreage is two acres or more, and this is just a bit less. So rather than give up their horses, they sold the property and moved elsewhere."

"Aunt Julie told us that this property had been vacant for quite a while before we bought it."

"Yes, that's another story. A woman in the States bought it unseen, but never moved in. Before she was able to come here, her parents had some medical issues and she left to be with them. It must have been serious because she never came back. Julie said she was paying someone to look after it but finally decided to sell it."

"Hard decisions to make," Peyton sighed. "Family comes first, of course, but sad for people to have to sell this beautiful property for those reasons. If I lived here, I would want some livestock." Tom frowned and cocked his head in confusion. "I love this place," Peyton explained, "but our plan is to renovate and then sell it again in a few months."

Tom's heart sank. He looked at her speculatively. "Really? I had no idea. You're going to be a house flipper? Are you sure you know what you are getting into? It's a tough business and this is a huge place."

Peyton stiffened and tossed her hair over her shoulder. "We know what we're doing. My father and I have purchased and renovated several homes in the last few years."

"I'm sorry," he said quickly. "I didn't mean to imply that you couldn't do it. It's just that a friend of mine tried to do the same thing, and he lost everything. His house turned out to have some terrible problems that he didn't find out about until he was in mid-reconstruction. He had to borrow heavily to finish the project, and then wasn't able sell the house a high enough price to pay off his loans. The family ended up bankrupt."

Peyton met his eyes. "I'm sorry about your friend. Of course, there are risks for any flip, and extensive home inspections are a must. But my dad is a contractor and we have our own company," she told him calmly. "This is what we do for a living. We're experienced and we know what we're doing."

"Oh well, then. I wish you all the best with this." The silence hung between them and he cleared his throat. "I'm sorry to hear, though, that you're only going to be here for a short time. How long does it usually take for you to complete a renovation project?"

"It depends on the building and how much work needs to be done. My dad figures we can get this one completed in about three months."

"Hmm…well, I hope you're able to make the most of your time here. You know what they say about all work and no play." That sounded a bit fresh, judging by Peyton's blush. "What I mean is, this town is a lovely place, people are very friendly, and we have fun activities all year round. The area has a great trail system too if you like hiking. There's a lot to be said for small communities, you know." He flashed a smile. "Only three traffic lights! Maybe you'll end up liking us so much that you won't want to go back to the big city," he teased.

Peyton managed a smile. "Oh, I doubt that. I've always been a city girl, born and bred. I love the Rockies though, and I'm hoping Dad and I will have some time to enjoy them. It was nice of you to bring the goodies. I really do appreciate it." Their eyes connected again and she was struck by their blue. With his thick black curls and his muscled arms, she realized he was very handsome.

Tom took the hint that it was time to go. He turned toward the door but then looked back at her. "Listen, since your dad isn't here yet, you might be a bit nervous staying alone here by yourself. I should give you my phone number in case you need anything. Remember, just around the curve. I can be here in minutes."

"Thank you, Tom, that's nice of you. It's good to have the connection. I'm sure my dad will appreciate meeting you too." She smiled and passed her phone for him to punch the numbers. "Thanks for the offer."

The corners of his eyes crinkled into a smile. "Welcome to the neighborhood." He turned at the door and met her eyes again. "You're very welcome. Good night, Peyton."

THREE

After more calls, trying again to reach Dave, Peyton gave up and went to bed, but couldn't sleep. Something was definitely wrong. It was not like him to fail keeping in touch. Tossing and turning, she didn't know what to do. She felt like calling Julie and Ed but couldn't, not in the middle of the night. Nothing could be done anyway until morning.

When the sun came up and she had made up her mind to call someone her phone rang and she saw Dave's name in the display. "Dad! I'm so relieved! Where are you?"

To her surprise, a woman's voice answered. "Hello, is this Peyton Carmichael?"

"Yes, who are you?"

"My name is Ellie and I'm calling from Sherbrook Hospital. Your dad asked me to call you."

Peyton felt faint and reached for a chair. "What? Dad is in the hospital? Is he alright?"

"He was in a vehicle crash last night and was brought here for treatment."

"Oh no! That's terrible! How was he hurt? Is he alright? Can I speak with him?"

"Not right now. He has been sedated, but he asked us to contact you, so you would know he's okay."

"Do you know what happened?"

"All we know is that last night, before he drove very far on his journey, he ran off the road into a ditch and hit a tree. He was brought back to the city by ambulance, injured but not for life threatening. I'm sorry, that's all I can tell you now. You'll be able to talk to him later and he'll give you more details."

Peyton hung up and began to shake, her eyes filled with tears. What should she do? She must go to him, to see for herself! Thank God he is okay! It could have been so much worse. He could have died. She must not panic. She took some deep breaths and eventually common sense prevailed, and she grabbed her phone and called Julie. She answered but said she was out of town and wouldn't be back until the next day. She promised to contact their church prayer chain and would come over as soon as she got back.

A few hours later the hospital nurse phoned again and Peyton was relieved to hear Dave's voice. "Hi, kitten," he croaked. He sounded terrible. "They finally let me call you."

"Oh, Dad! Tears were running down her cheeks. "How are you? I was so scared when the nurse called me earlier. What happened?"

"Someone was passing me on a curve and forced me to take the shoulder. I ran off the road and into a huge tree. The truck didn't roll over but it really smashed hard. The front of the truck pushed back into the front seat. My legs were caught in the mess and I was knocked out cold. The pick-up is toast, I'm afraid."

"Wow! The nurse said they were taking x-rays this morning. Have you been given the results? Do you know what they found?"

"My left leg is okay. Apparently, the driver-side door popped open and didn't get crunched much. Hurts bad right now, but it's just bruises. My right leg was what took most of the force. I had to be cut out of the truck by firemen and pulled out through the windshield. My right leg is broken in two places. Apparently, I will have to have surgery at some point."

Peyton was dismayed but gulped down her tears. She had to be strong so her dad wouldn't worry. But surgery! This must be serious. People with leg injuries could have blood clots that would be fatal. "Oh, Dad…I'm so sorry this happened. I'll pack up the motorhome and come home as soon as I can."

"No, honey…. I 've been thinking about that. You need to stay. Someone has to be at the site." He paused to take some breaths. "Apparently the hospital is bringing in an orthopedic specialist. I was told they will insert a rod in my leg put screws at my knee and ankle." There was a slight pause and then he dropped the bombshell. "I'm so sorry, sweetie. This is really going to mess up our house flip. I'll be laid up for at least six to eight weeks, maybe more with physiotherapy. I want you to start on the reno's yourself. You must find a local contractor there to work with you."

"Dad, I don't care about the flip. I want to be there to look after you. Why don't I just lock up the Lodge and we'll wait for a couple of months until you get better? I can't do this on my own!"

"No can do, Kitten. The bank has given us a line of credit for three months so we have a deadline to keep. The contracts have been made, the materials have been ordered, and trucks will soon be coming to the site. We've gone too far now to pull back. You should be able to find some workers there to help you with the job. I'm sure Julie and Ed will know of some. I'm not sure how long I'll be in the hospital, but we can keep in touch by phone and video chat, and as soon as I'm fit to travel, I'll come. I'm counting on you, Peyton. You need to do this for me… for us."

Peyton could hear the pain in his voice and her eye's eyes filled with tears again. "Okay, Dad." She could hear a nurse in the background, whispering "enough for now". "I'm sure everything will be fine. Will you have the hospital call me after the surgery to tell me how it went? And don't worry. I'll make things work on our end. Just get well. I love you, Dad. I'll be praying for you."

After hanging up, Peyton began to panic. They had done many flips together but Dave was always the one in charge. And she knew this project would take far more time than just few weeks. It was a huge responsibility. She felt like screaming! *God, why is this happening? Where do I even start?*

After a few minutes of heavy breathing, her heartbeat got back to normal. She knew that her aunt and uncle could be counted on to help her through this. She would call them in the morning and start the ball rolling. She wouldn't let her father down.

It had been exhausting …. unpacking and cleaning all day at the Lodge, worrying for her dad's arrival, and now this news. She sank into bed. It had been several years since she had really prayed for something. Prayers for her mother when she was so sick, and in so much pain from the cancer, had not helped to save her life. Dave and Peyton had both felt a bitterness and prayers were forgotten then, but God still loved them.

Thank you, God for protecting Dad and keeping him safe. It could have been much worse…he could have been killed. Thank you for the nurses and doctors who are bringing him through this. And thank you for my family here. I know I can rely on them to help me make the right decisions for what lies ahead. Please give me the strength I need to do this, Lord. I know I haven't talked to you for a long time but I really need you now.

FOUR

After the evening with the church event, Tom put his truck in gear and drove home, silently berating himself. He had just been introduced to the prettiest girl he had met in a long time, and he shouldn't have ruffled her feathers by being so quick to criticize. He had only been trying to help, but she probably thought he was a know-it-all. He was intrigued at the thought of having Peyton and her dad as neighbors, even if it was only for a short time. He respected the fact that they were successful house flippers, and it would be interesting to see what they would do to upgrade the Lodge. Peyton didn't look like someone who worked in construction, though. He chuckled as he pictured the petite brunette swinging a hammer or bashing down a wall. He wondered if he should offer his services to help. Might be a good way to get to know her better, without coming on too strong. He had his own construction business but maybe he could spare some of his crew to help these folks with their project. He'd offer to work for free, but if she insisted on paying him, that would work too. The missions fund could stand a bit of bolstering.

Unlike most young boys learning skills from their fathers, Tom lost that when his father Peter abandoned his family. At the time, he was fourteen years old and his younger brother Allen was ten. They never saw or heard from their dad again. To be able to survive, their mother Helen worked long hours at a local convenience store, and her sons did odd jobs after school. Money was always in short supply but they managed somehow. The boys were fortunate to have an and mentor Ed who took the boys under his wing. He was a carpenter by trade himself and opened his shop and his heart to the boys. After high school, Tom's mother Helen had insisted that he go on to a technical school and to please her, he did a few courses at college. But his passion was for woodworking, and Ed encouraged him to apprentice with a local home-builders company that specialized in log home builds. He learned from the best, and after several years started his own business. He helped to support his mother but Allen went another way and had very little contact with them. When he did, it was usually to ask for money.

As he pulled into his own driveway, Tom saw his golden retriever Carver loping down the lane towards him. The motion light came on and Tom parked the truck, then stopped to stroke the dog's ears before entering the house. He loved his log home, but tonight it had an empty feeling. Lately he had been aware of the young couples at his church, the closeness they had with one another, and the joy they shared with their children. A kinship that spoke of deep commitment and lasting love, something Tom was beginning to long for. He had been a bachelor for a long time and it was time for him to find a partner and family.

His thoughts were for Peyton. He had gone out with several women over the years, avoiding the ones that he would have been ashamed to introduce to his mother, but none seem to really click with him. He had a relationship with the Lord and he needed someone who fulfilled his life intellectually, emotionally, and spiritually. Now pretty Peyton had come on the scene and she interested him. He wished she had come to the church social. She had a beauty and wholesomeness that attracted him, and he would like to know her better.

Early the next day Julie and Ed came out to the Lodge. Julie brought a lunch basket, and over coffee, hugs and tears, Peyton she told them about Dave's accident and that he wanted her to start work on the Lodge without him. They were sympathetic but firmly optimistic that Peyton had the ability to handle the job. After all, she was a Journeyman carpenter and had been working alongside of her dad for years, building beautiful homes and renovating other buildings. This one would be her finest accomplishment, and her family promised they would do everything they could to help.

Julie called Tom to tell him about Dave's crash. He was shocked and came right over to the Lodge, concerned about the accident and how bad it was, and wondering how Peyton was taking it. He immediately offered to help with the project as much as he could. He was known to be a good Samaritan in town and help others, and now was a time when he was needed.

Peyton had done a lot of thinking and praying overnight and was now much calmer. She still needed to plan how she was going to handle things, though. She knew she would have to swallow her pride to hire local workers and was glad when Julie suggested bringing Tom and Ed into the picture. They were both good men and had experience from building their own homes with beautiful results. Ed was retired and was glad to be offered the opportunity.

Dave was upset that he could not be part of it all, but

Peyton promised that after the surgery was successful and he was out of the hospital, they would keep in touch to reassure him things were going well. He hoped to come to the site, but Peyton thought it best that he be cautious. An accident like this must have upset his whole body, and he needed to let things heal slowly. Worrying about the project wouldn't help either. During the month before, Dave and Peyton had discussed what renovations were to be made, so she knew what to do. If there were any serious glitches that needed her dad's attention, they could discuss with him online.

Peyton was surprised and intrigued when Tom told her about his log homes company. He had four homes under construction at his yard but said he would gladly spare a few of his employees to help at the Lodge. Tom and Peyton took some time to draw up a schedule for extra workers a few days of the week and occasional Saturdays if needed. No Sundays, though, and Peyton respected him for that, remembering his commitment to his church.

When everyone had finished eating, she took them on a complete tour of the Lodge, right up to the third floor which was large and gloomy and had obviously not been used for years. Peyton planned to put a master bedroom and ensuite up there, as well as a small office. Right now, the space was dusty and full of junk - trunks, boxes of papers, old clothes and shoes, outdated ski equipment and much more. Probably a lot of spiders and other critters hiding in there too, but the good news was that there were no signs of any ceiling leaks, and there were four good size windows, in good shape.

Just to be sure the building was habitable Peyton would contact a HAZMAT asbestos specialist to investigate the Lodge the next day. If all was well, they could begin work. So much to do! She had drawn new blueprints for the second and third floors to create bedrooms with ensuites, and would start framing the third-floor master suite rooms. Tom's crew would be dispatched to the other floors to start ripping up old rugs, baseboards and floor tiles. Eventually others would start demolishing in the kitchen, banging out cabinets and countertops and pushing out walls to make room for larger fixtures.

With plans in place for his crew to start the upcoming Monday, Tom asked Peyton to wish Dave a speedy recovery and took his leave. Peyton called Dave to see how he was and told him what was happening. "What do you think, Dad? Tom seems to be a good guy, very experienced and a hard worker. You know what? He says he doesn't want to be put on the payroll for his work, just his employees. Helping a neighbor, he said, but I insisted on a business relationship, and told him we will pay him the same amount as we do other employees."

"Yes, you must do that. I'm impressed. What a guy! He must be very knowledgeable, if he owns and operates a log home company. I think he's just what we need. I sure wish I could be there with you, honey. hm so angry with myself for lousing up this project. I should have been more careful, a better driver."

"Dad, please don't beat yourself up about that. You are an excellent driver and it was the other guy that was to blame. Did the police ever find out who it was?"

"No and I couldn't give them a description of the driver or the vehicle. I was trying not to roll the truck. I managed to keep it upright in the ditch, and if I hadn't hit that big tree, I probably could have driven out again." His voice dropped. "I'm really sorry now that we decided to do this flip."

She was surprised at the response that came to her mind, but it was true. "You know, Dad…I'm not. I'm very sorry that you had the accident and were injured, but I think an angel was there in the truck with you. Things could have been so much worse. God allowed this to happen for a reason. It may not make sense to us now, but perhaps further on it will." Her thoughts went to the folks that were supporting them - Julie and Ed, and Tom and his crew. "Maybe we're a blessing to these folks too, who knows?"

Dave sighed. "You may be right, honey. I just feel so frustrated for leaving you with all this responsibility. You shouldn't have to do this on your own."

"I'm not alone, Dad. Things are set up now and I have capable employees that help me with the project. And perhaps when you get better, you'll be able to come and see for yourself. Now I'd better let you go because I can hear from your voice that you're getting tired. I love you, Dad. Please don't worry about anything. I'll be in touch again soon."

After signing off, Peyton began to relax and realize that she finally believed in herself. Everything was going to be all right. She would miss having Dave at the project but knew that she had enough skilled people to back her up. She thought about working with Tom and felt confident that with his expertise, they all could work well together as a team.

Thoughts of him swelled up, remembering when they met, and how insistent Julie had been that she get to know him. If Julie thought that much of him, he must be a good man. She would have many opportunities to get to know him during the weeks ahead, and she wondered where that would take them both. Time would tell!

You know this is only a business relationship and you need to stick to it. Friendly, friends...but certainly not anything more. When this project is finished, you must go back to the city. Guard your heart!

FIVE

After a good night sleep in the motorhome, Peyton felt refreshed and eager to start work. Dave had asked that she make a trip into town to visit local businesses that he had arranged contracts with on their first visit to the town – lumber yards, hardware stores, electricians, and plumbers. The delivery trucks that he had arranged for would not be arriving yet, and it would be fun to explore the small town. Why not? She could take a bit of time to enjoy the place before they began the hard work.

She was surprised how pretty the town was, with spring flower baskets hanging from street corner lamps and murals painted on the sides of several buildings. She popped into the various stores Dave had visited and told them what had happened. Everyone was sympathetic and wished her well. At the lumber yard the manager was particularly friendly. "You know, having the Lodge open again is going to be really good for our town. You folks are purchasing so much for the renovations that our local stores will be getting the most business we've had in a long time. Years ago, this town was a busy place, bustling with people, both summer and winter. But then the Lodge shut down and tourists had nowhere to stay. It really affected the whole town. Once the Lodge gets finished and open for business, we're expecting a lot of tourists coming this way. We want to see that happen so please let us know if there's anything we can do to help." Peyton reassured the owners that the deliveries would arrive soon and mentioned that Tom would be helping with the project. The reaction was extremely positive. It was obvious that he was well-known and respected in this town.

Wandering around, she stopped at the local hospital auxiliary thrift shop, buying a few things she didn't really need but happy to support. She loved the little antique shop too and admired many things but came out with only a small wooden sign reading, "No Such Thing as Too Many Books." Julie's realty office was just down the street from where Peyton had parked her motorhome, so she returned their crock pot, and offered to buy her lunch, an offer Julie accepted delightedly. Afterwards Julie took her on a stroll around town and they sat on a bench at the Rotary Park in the sunshine. Mothers were chatting with friends and watching their children play.

Of course, Julie wanted to talk about Tom's visit the day before. Peyton sighed. "Yes, he was very nice, wasn't he? To supply us with some of his own employees."

"He's promised to help you when he can afford to get away from his own business. That's a good sign, don't you think?"

"Of what, Auntie?"

"That he really likes you. I knew he would want to help in your project."

"I'm thankful that he's going to take part, Auntie, but don't get your hopes up. I admit he is very generous. And yes, he is good looking. But please don't try to matchmake. I have no intention of getting involved with a man now. There's going to be a lot to do, and we only have three months. Once this flip is finished, we have to go back to the big city."

Julie smiled and raised her eyebrows, squeezing Peyton's hand. She knew better. She could already tell that Tom was interested in her lovely niece, and she would do everything she could to make the weeks ahead a sign for the future.

The next day, Tom arrived at the Lodge right on time, with some equipment and a few crew members. The Lodge had passed the Hazmat test, and Peyton had cleaned up the loft and taped off areas of the master suite and office. A truck full of lumber had arrived from the city so she and Tom decided to start their work on the third floor with two young helpers. Two others were dispatched to the second floor to start removing old baseboards and carpets. She was impressed with Tom's attention to detail and the care he took to protect the walls and floors. He seemed to take a genuine interest in the Lodge and her plans for it. Peyton talked about washing walls and doing some painting on her own time, but Tom was wary. He'd privately decided to give her as much of his time as possible. He didn't like the idea of her up on a ladder with no one around.

They worked in companionable silence at first and it wasn't long before they began chatting and learning more about one another. Peyton asked Tom if he had always lived in the area.

"Born and bred. My parents moved here forty years ago, when the pulp mill was built. My dad worked there for twenty of those years." Something in his voice suggested he didn't like talking about it.

"Do your parents still live here?'

"My mom does. My dad left us when I was fourteen. Haven't seen him since."

"Oh, I'm so sorry, Tom. I shouldn't have brought it up."

"That's all right. My mother's worth ten of him. She was a stay-at-home mom until she lost Dad's income, so she found a job, and has worked at the same corner store for over fifteen years." He smiled fondly. "She worked so hard and did such a good job that the elderly owner left the store to her in his will. She still owns and works there. She is an amazing lady. Almost everyone in town knows and loves my mom."

"Are you an only child?"

"No, I have a younger brother, Allen. He doesn't live here now, though. He kind of went his own way when he graduated and doesn't come home very much. To be honest with you, I'm not even sure where he's living right now. I don't know...we're afraid he's into drugs." He shook his head. "It bothers Mom a lot to think he's strayed so far from the way he was brought up."

"That's sad," Peyton sighed. "I'm an only child. Always wished I had a brother."

"I can see that you and your dad are close."

"Yes, we've always been. When I was growing up, I wanted to be a teacher like my mom. My dad worked at construction and spent a lot of his free time working in the garage at home. I loved to hang out there especially when he was working with wood. He helped me make things like bird houses and other small projects, and he wasn't afraid to try anything. One time he designed and made a tent trailer, and another time a 14-foot boat. When I was in high school and other kids were taking cooking classes, I took carpentry. My industrial arts teacher encouraged me to apply for an apprenticeship, and because my dad was a contractor, I was able to get into a program through him." Peyton's voice wavered a bit. "Unfortunately, that year my mom was diagnosed with cancer, and given only four to six months to live. I decided right then that I would put my plans aside. Turned out she lived a full year, and the three of us were able to spend a lot of quality time together, doing things that she had always wanted to do, going places that she had always wanted to see. She made a 'Bucket List' and checked off each thing, one by one, until she no longer could leave her bed. Dad and I tried to do it all, but it was impossible. It slowed down my career plans but I wouldn't trade those precious times for anything. I still miss her every day."

Tom listened quietly, noting the tears she was blinking away. After a few moments, he cleared his throat. "My story is a bit different. My dad was a great guy, and we were close when I was young, although that changed when I was in my teens. For some reason, he became different - harsh about everything I did. Mom noticed it and tried to talk to him but it didn't help. That only made it worse. He made me feel like he loved Allen more than he loved me. It seemed that everything I wanted to do, he was against. He was a salesman but he wanted me to be scholarly, educated, cultured. That's not at all what I wanted, and he couldn't accept it. I just wanted to work with wood, making beautiful things. Being anything else was inconceivable to me – still is. I wish he could see some of the work I've done. But one day I came home from school and found my mother weeping. Dad had left us without even saying goodbye."

Peyton felt her heart melting for him. "I'm so sorry, Tom. Losing someone is a blow. Something we will never forget. I'm sure he would be proud of you now. So far, I've only met a few people in this town, but I've heard them praise you, not just about your work at the log yard but in the community. They respect you. I'd love to see some of the other things you've created one of these days. I was told that they are lovely." She stood up then, feeling a bit uncomfortable at feelings that were surfacing. She cleared her throat. "Guess we should keep going so that we can finish before nightfall."

SIX

B y evening, Tom and Peyton had made a good start on the top floor and he headed for home. He had enjoyed working with Peyton and didn't relish going home to his empty house. Julie had phoned and invited Tom and Peyton to dinner, but Peyton quickly declined, so Tom did as well. He suspected Julie wanted a run-down of the day they had spent together, and he wasn't about to give her the satisfaction. Anyway, he had to take the dog for a run, then drop by the church to help with the youth group tonight like he usually did.

Thinking about Peyton, he felt that things had shifted for her at the end of their lunch break. And he wasn't sure why. She seemed subdued for the rest of the afternoon. Perhaps talking about her mother's death had upset her but he thought it was more than that. She was polite but there was coolness in her demeanor that puzzled him. With a sigh, he maneuvered his pickup out of the driveway and drove the short distance to his home, where he was surprised to find a car parked in front of the double garage doors. He stifled a groan. He knew only too well who the vehicle belonged to.

"Hello, Tom! I thought you would never get here. I've been waiting for hours." A blond woman met him at the truck door with outstretched arms. Her hair was long and curly, and she was dressed in a low-cut top, tight jeans, and spike heels, and wore a heavy layer of make-up. Tom felt disgusted.

"Tracey. What on earth are you doing here?" He side-stepped the hug and frowned at the young woman. "A long way from home, aren't you?"

"I came to visit you, Tom. Aren't you glad to see me?" She made a pout and reached out to rub his arm. "I've missed you. Will you invite me in?"

"I have nothing to say to you. The last time we were together, you made it clear that you didn't want anything more to do with me. Is your husband with you?"

"Oh, we broke up ages ago," she sighed. "He just wasn't the right guy for me. Too many issues." She looked up at him through heavy mascara. "I guess I didn't know what a good thing I had when you and I were together."

"Look, Tracey," Tom began. "I've had a long day and I'm tired and hungry. Say what you have to."

"Well, for starters, I need a place to stay for the night. I didn't like the looks of any of the motels I passed coming into town. I'd much prefer to stay in your lovely home."

"That's not going to happen," Tom said firmly, as he unlocked the door. Carver, a huge yellow retriever burst out of the house and jumped joyously at the newcomer, knocking her against her car and splashing a nearby puddle.

"Get him off me! Look what he's done to my clothes! Whatever possesses you to have such a big dog?"

Tom collared Carver and rubbed his ears fondly. "Listen, he just happens to be my best friend and he's been in my family for a long time. Go for a run, boy, go on!" The huge dog sped away and Tom turned his attention to Tracey. "Okay, what do you want? I have plans for this evening and I'm running late."

Tracey brushed by him and sailed into his house. "What a nice home you have, Tom! Did you build it? Not the style I would prefer though." She plopped down on the couch and gazed around the open living space. "I need a rest. Surely you can at least offer me a cup of coffee, Tom. I'd like to catch up." He bit his tongue and resisted the urge to reply that he had no interest in catching up with a girlfriend that had run off with his best friend five years ago.

Tom popped a coffee pod into the machine and pressed the button. If giving her a quick coffee would get rid of her, he'd do it. "Why are you here, Tracey? We haven't seen each other for years. I can't imagine why you think I would be glad to see you after what you did to me."

Tracey opened her mouth to protest but hesitated a moment. "That was a long time ago, Tom. We were young. Maybe I did make a mistake back then."

"You thought you'd hit the jackpot when you decided to marry Barrett." "What happened with him?"

"He wasn't the man I thought he was. We split up several years after graduation. I did my best to stay but we were just not compatible. He wanted a family and I couldn't bear the thought, at least not yet. I have much more to see and do before I have to get tied down with children." She looked at him sideways and smiled coyly. "Surely you understand, Tom, don't you? You're still single from what I hear."

"Single by choice, Tracey. I happen to believe that God has a soulmate for me and that in due time, if it is His will, I'll meet her. I don't want to run ahead of what He plans for me. I trust Him."

"Still on that religious kick, Tom? Seriously, how can you believe that? Don't talk to me about God's plan." She looked away for a moment and when she looked back, her eyes were wet. "I need help right now, Tom. My money's running out and I can't get back home. I barely have enough money for gas."

"Where is home now, Tracey?" She was silent and looked at him with tears in her eyes. "I'm not sure. When I left Barrett, he sold our condo and I went back to our family home. I thought I could still live there but my parents are hardly around. Because of their business, they do a lot of travelling all over the world. Most of the time just the housekeeper Marie is there, and she hates me. When Mom and Dad do come home, all we do is argue. Marie tells lies about me that aren't true. She doesn't want me to live there anymore. And they assume I still have my grandparents' trust money and can live on that. I called our lawyer about it today and he says it's all gone, and apparently my parents told him they aren't going to support me anymore. They want me to get a job and start living on my own. What am I going to do? I'm completely broke."

"I'm sorry, Tracey. My first thought is that you should sell your car. Is it your own or is it a rental?"

"It is mine and I'm not selling it. I can't do that. Period."

Tom sighed. "Listen…I'm busy tonight and need to leave pretty quick. We can meet tomorrow and talk some more, but you can't stay here tonight. Can't you go back to your parents?"

"Marie locked me out last night and I slept in my car."

"That's terrible! Well, a friend of mine owns a motel here. I'll give him a call and get you a room for the night. And we'll talk about it again tomorrow. Let's go. You can follow me."

"Thank you, Tom." Tracey sighed and pulled herself off the couch. "I'm sorry to bother you with all this. I don't know anyone else to turn to. I'll be around for a while. Maybe move back here permanently." That remark made Tom groan inwardly.

Tracey wasn't keen about Tom stopping off at the church but she had no choice. Teenagers were waiting outside the door. Surprisingly she seemed to enjoy watching the basketball game and sat chatting with some of the girls there. Tom was a bit worried that people would think Tracey was his girlfriend, and sure enough, the guys teased him about it afterward. Tracy loved the attention but Tom gritted his teeth. "Just an old friend," he stated. "Visiting from out of town."

After a rigorous hour spent playing basketball with the church youth, Tom felt better. Tracey followed him to his friend's motel and Tom paid Andre to registered her for a week. Maybe she would be able to find work by then, although he doubted it. In all the years he had known her, she had been a spoiled brat and expected everyone else to do things for her.

Tracey had been his girlfriend years ago when they were in high school. From the beginning, her parents did not approve of him. They were a very wealthy family and after dating her for a while, he came to realize they lived in different worlds. Tracey's home was a mansion in the most expensive neighborhood in town. Tom came from a single parent family who struggled to pay the rent most of the time. She loved to go to events where she could wear beautiful clothes and socialize with rich people. Tom didn't even own a suit and preferred to hang out with less affluent friends that went to the movies on dates, or played outdoor sports in the park. She was born with a sliver spoon in her mouth, as the saying goes. Tom worked hard at two jobs to help his mother put food on the table and raise his younger brother. After graduation, Tracey wanted him to go to the same prestigious college as she did. Tom had no money or desire to get more education, and instead found a mentor who helped him start his own business as a log home builder. Not surprisingly, their paths diverted and they went their own ways. Tracey chose a rich boyfriend and turned her nose up at Tom's plans. He wasn't heartbroken at all. In fact, had he been relieved to see her go. But now she was back in his life and he wasn't happy at all.

SEVEN

After two weeks in hospital, Dave's doctor agreed to discharge him, providing he had someone to care for him at home. While he was puzzling how he could do that, the head nurse, Ellie Mitchell, who had been on duty when he was brought in after the accident, poked her head in to say goodbye.

"Going home today, Dave! That's good news. For the first week or two, the hospital has arranged for a home care nurse to come daily to check your vitals and have a look at your leg. And I've assured the doctor that you'll have more support at home. We've arranged for someone to come a couple of times a week to look after your house, and I have a list of people who volunteered to check on you regularly, in person or by phone. Plus, the church ladies will make sure you have a hot meal each evening for the next two weeks, longer if necessary. Now Pastor Bob will be by to pick you up shortly. How does that sound?"

Dave's eyes moistened and he was speechless for a moment. "I can't believe this. I haven't been in church for several years," he mumbled. Why would people be so good to me?"

"God has not forgotten you, Dave, and neither have your brothers and sisters in Christ. You've been on the

41

church prayer list ever since your wife first got sick. Now it is our pleasure to show our love to you and Peyton in a more tangible way."

Just then Pastor Bob poked his head around the corner. "Hey, buddy. Your chariot has arrived!" He and Dave shook hands and the pastor sat down on the bed for a moment. "Good to see you, man! You've had quite a time, haven't you?"

"Yeah, it's been a struggle this past two weeks." Dave briefly shared what had happened with the accident and the fact that Peyton was over 300 miles away at the flip house. The pastor shook his head in in admiration that she would agree to start the reno's on her own. "That's my girl," Dave said. "Always up for a challenge. But I'm starting to feel better now. I hope to be able to join her there soon."

"Well, I know how you feel but take it easy. You need to make sure that leg is mended before you go too far. I'm going to make the rounds to say hello to a few other church members that are also in hospital, but I'll be done in a half hour or so. Sound good? I'm sure you'll be glad to go home."

"You bet! I'll be ready for you."" Dave swung his leg onto the floor and gingerly began to get dressed. These last few days, he had practiced walking with crutches provided by the nurses. Thank God his injuries had not been as serious as was first thought, although his right leg now had a couple of pins in it.

On the way home, Pastor Bob stopped at a local medical equipment shop so Dave could rent a wheelchair and another pair of crutches, since the others had to be returned to the hospital. His home was a level-entry rancher, so it would be easy to navigate at home. When they arrived and Dave was settled in, Pastor Bob made a pot of coffee for them and spent another hour chatting with him about the accident and the plans for the new project. He was very interested in Peyton since he'd known her since she was a child. "She used to love coming to church, right from her Sunday School days. Even in her teen years she attended church faithfully."

Dave hung his head and frowned. "Things changed when Melisa got cancer. We were devastated and almost lost the business. Peyton and I wanted to be with her mom as much as we could. Church just didn't seem important anymore. It was a rough time for all of us."

They had a time of prayer together, asking God for Dave's return to physical health, and the strength for Peyton to do the tasks she had before her. When Pastor Bob got up to leave, Dave asked, "Does the church still have the Handy-bus running? I think I'd like to have them pick me up for a Sunday service once I feel a bit better." Pastor Bob smiled broadly and pulled out a pen and pocket pad. "They certainly do, Dave. I'll give you the number to call. We'd love to see you."

After the pastor departed, Dave phoned Peyton and filled her in. "I still can't believe the church stepped up to help me so much. I can't remember the last time we even went to a service."

"I know, Dad. I've been thinking about how God protected you during the accident and how it could have been so much worse." Peyton swallowed hard while her eyes moistened. "I'm so grateful that you were spared. I don't know what I would have done if I'd lost you too."

"I know, Kitten, I know. But I'm safe now and feeling much better. I won't be able to drive for a while though, and I need to stick around for some follow-up appointments with the Doc. But I'll be fine in a few weeks and on my way back to you."

Peyton detected a note of weariness in his voice. Time to hang up. She was glad that her dad was feeling so cheerful, and happy to link up with the church again. But resentment was still in her heart for the way her mother had been taken away from them in such a painful way. It was hard for her to understand why God would let that happen. It would take a long time for her to feel comfortable in the church again.

EIGHT

For the next few weeks, everything was busy at the Lodge site. The rooms up in the loft were now framed and walled up with Gyproc, ready for paint and tiles. The electricians and plumbers had finished up there and were now working on the second floor. Knocking out walls in the former master suite, bathrooms and other bedrooms, the area was now several smaller rooms. When all was done, there would be eight units on that floor, each with an ensuite.

Tom and Peyton were at somewhat of a stalemate for the work on the second floor. The flooring in the rooms and hallway had been torn up and disposed of, but until the framing was complete and the wiring in place, the walls couldn't go up. The gutting of the bathrooms was done, and they were waiting for more materials and fixtures to be delivered from the city. Together Tom and Peyton had planned the new kitchen layout and would soon begin constructing the boxes of the cupboards. The pre-made cupboard doors and countertops would arrive in another shipment within a couple of weeks.

Working alongside Peyton the past few weeks, Tom couldn't help but notice that she was certainly a professional and experienced renovator. He admired her work ethic and respected the way she took charge of his crew to direct what she wanted done. At the same time, she was open to comments and suggestions. Her cheerful nature and enthusiasm for the project created a work atmosphere that made them all feel respected and valued. Peyton, on the other hand, noticed how good Tom was to his employees, more like a comrade than a boss, friendly and respectful but firm when necessary. The workers were charmed by Peyton and eager to please her, and there was no flirting, impropriety or cussing allowed on site.

Tom and Peyton's friendship had been growing as they worked alongside one another, despite Peyton's resolve to keep everything business-like. She loved the way Tom acted with the men, and that extended to her. She couldn't help but notice his easy smile and how handsome he was. She looked forward to seeing him each day that he came, and her heart always lifted when she heard his voice.

Dave seemed to like him as well. His trust in Tom increased, even if they were online, and the frequency of their video chats was a Godsend. Although Dave longed to help them work on the renovations, he had grown to rely on both Peyton and Tom's judgements.

One morning, the crew was assigned to pull up all the carpets in the living and dining rooms. Jerry, the electrician had arrived and was having a coffee with Tom and Peyton on the front porch. "What a beautiful piece of property, Peyton! I've driven past here quite a few times but never really noticed it much. I hear you're going to sell it when it's all done." He chuckled. "Maybe I'll buy it!"

"Well, that's the plan. Get out your wallet!" Peyton looked around ruefully. "It's so awesome, I'd love to live here myself. Such beauty and peace compared to the city."

"Why don't you?" Jerry smiled at her. "It would be a great place to raise a family. Do you know, it's less than a 20-minute drive to the National Park? A wonderful area. Lots of opportunities for mountain climbing, hiking, camping, skiing…even stargazing! Our town is a designated Dark Sky Place and there's a festival each year for that. We've had millions of people come here, and numerous professional astronauts as guests."

"Sounds wonderful," Peyton sighed. "I've always lived in the big city and you can't see any stars at all because of all those lights." She stole a glance at Tom who was watching her intently and felt herself blushing. "Maybe I'll come back for a holiday sometime."

When Jerry went inside, Peyton turned to Tom. "Before I forget, I wanted to ask you something. The grass in the yard is getting very long. There's a lawn tractor in the barn that was left here by the previous owners. Not sure if it works. When you get a chance, could you please look and help me get it started? "

"Sure thing. How about right now?" He led the way to the rear of the property. "I see what you mean. You need some goats or a pony to keep that pasture under control," he teased. "Oh, I forgot, no livestock allowed." Such a shame, she thought. Kids would love that. She felt a twinge of sadness. She was getting more and more attached to this piece of real estate.

"Wow! Look at that! Nice big garden patch. Though I'm not sure how much could be grown there, with the deer and elk population we have passing through. They're pretty to watch but without some high fencing around it, at least ten feet, they would eat everything."

"In the city, it's rabbits we have to worry about. I love them, personally, but my mom had an awful time keeping them out of our yard. Eventually she gave up and planted nasturtiums instead. I was told they're peppery and the wildlife don't like them." She swallowed. "We haven't had a garden since Mom died."

"Do you live with your dad in the city, or do you have your own apartment?"

"I've lived in our family home ever since I was born. I was thinking of getting my own place when I was finished my apprenticeship, but then Mom got sick and everything changed." Peyton kept walking but fumbled for a tissue in her pocket. "My dad built our house when I was just a child and continued to build for others down through the years. When Mom got cancer, he stopped taking big jobs, so he could help me care for her." Peyton swallowed the lump in her throat that always came when she thought of those days. "When she died, he just fell apart. He became horridly depressed and started to drink heavily. He didn't want to work at all for a quite a while, and the bills piled up. I understood how he felt but I was hurting too. It got to the point where I felt I should get a different kind of job and move out on my own. When I suggestion that to him, it was kind of a wake-up call, and he realized what he was doing. He stopped drinking entirely, and we began to enjoy each other again. We started work and things got better. Then one day, when we were watching a TV show about house remodeling, he said "That's what I want to do! And he came to life." She smiled through the mist. "We've been flipping homes ever since."

Tom reached across and squeezed her hand. "I'm so sorry about your mom. It must have been very hard for you both."

"It was. She suffered so much that it was a blessing when she finally passed away. We couldn't wish her back, and we know she is in a better place now."

Tom found the latch on the barn door and swung it open wide. It was empty except for the lawn tractor and a fuel jug. Surprisingly, it was full. Tom gave the machine a once-over and checked the fuel level, topped it off and pronounced that everything looked fine. Peyton produced the key from her pocket and Tom folded his long legs into the seat. After a few attempts, the engine came to life. Loud but functional. Peyton breathed a sigh of relief. Having to mow the grass on the acreage with a regular mower would have taken forever.

Tom showed Peyton how to drive the tractor and lower the cutting blade. They had a few laughs when she drove it around a bit to get used to it. Then he motioned for her to stop and kill the engine. "Hey, I just had a great idea!" He had a big smile on his face. "A proposition for you. I happen to know a kid that comes to our church youth group who got himself into a bit of trouble, hanging out with the wrong guys. He has some community hours that he needs to work off, judge's order. I bet he would love to come out here and mow your lawn."

"Hmm." Peyton was cautious. "I'm not sure I want a troubled teenager on our worksite. We have enough to do as it is, without having to monitor him."

"He's a really good kid, Peyton. His name is Jason Taylor. I'm sure you would like him. I know his parents and they're good people. This is the first time he's been in trouble and it was a just lapse in judgement. But the Court has a bunch of hours he must work off within the next three months. He could probably do some other small jobs around the site as well. What do you say?"

Peyton looked at his earnest face and had to smile. "Well…okay. I trust your judgement, Tom. But he can only come on the days you're here to supervise him. Deal?"

"Deal! Tell you what. Jason and his parents come to church every week. Why don't you come with me this

Sunday and I'll introduce you? Julie and Ed will be there and my mother too. I'd really like you to meet her."

"Oh, I don't know about that. I'd like to meet your mom, but I haven't got Sunday clothes. And I haven't been to a church for a long time."

"We're country folks and people wear whatever they want to, so don't worry about that. Our church is small and everyone is friendly. I'm sure you'll be comfortable. After the service we have a coffee time, so we can talk with Jason's parents and make arrangements for him to start work." Peyton hesitated but Tom was so earnest, she gave in. "That's great!" He grinned and grabbed her in a hug. "Thanks, Peyton…you won't be sorry."

The hug was a bit of a shock. She hadn't had a hug from a guy for a long time and it felt good, although she knew she was blushing. Tom's face flushed too, as he realized what he'd done. For a breathless moment his eyes caught hers and then he turned away. "Doing this for Jason could make a huge difference in his life, you know. Thank you so much, Peyton!"

NINE

Realizing that he had been devoting a lot of time from his own business to help Peyton, Tom headed for his business site the next morning. Crews were working on different areas of the site, and a particular home structure had already been erected with numbered logs, then dismantled and transferred to flatbed trucks that would be going to Oregon, USA. A contractor there would have prepared the foundation, and when they arrive, Tom's crew would painstakingly reassemble the logs. Once that was done, the customer would be responsible for adding the roof, windows and doors, and interior rooms.

Tom was pleased with the work that was being done and spent the morning in his office catching up with paperwork. Just as his stomach was telling him it was time for a lunch break, his secretary opened the door and poked her head in. "Chief, you have some visitors!" Tom looked up and was shocked to see his brother Allen at the door, with a young woman and baby in her arms. He felt a pang of dismay! He hadn't seen Allen for over a year, and the last time they were at odds with one another. What was going to happen now?

Allen smiled and stretched out his hand. "Hi, Brother! Can we interrupt you for a few minutes?"

Tom stood up to reach across the desk. He didn't quite

know what to say. "Well isn't this a surprise! Good to see you. It's been a long time."

"Yeah, it sure is. I'm sorry, Tom. I should have kept in better touch with you. This is my fiancé Charlene, and our daughter, Jasmine."

"Wow!" Tom came around and smiled at the young woman. She smiled back and turned the baby so he could see her. "Allen! You're a dad now? That's amazing! Are you just visiting, or what?"

"At the moment, we're staying at the Timberland Inn. We've decided to move back home, Tom. Now that we're a family, it seems like a good place to raise our little girl."

Tom came around the desk and took the baby's perfect little hand in his. A flashback reminded him of the last time he'd seen Allen, who was high on drugs then. He searched Allen's face for any signs but saw that he and his fiancé looked healthy, happy and proud of their lovely child.

"Does Mom know you're back?" Tom asked. Allen had been a heartache for his mom when he was a teenager. He knew his mother would be thrilled to know she had a grandchild.

"Yeah, we just came from the store. "Allen chuckled. "She was so excited! She had customers clustered around to see Jasmine."

Tom was skeptical but tried not to show it. "Well! This is great, folks." He cleared his throat. "Have you guys had lunch? I was just going to get a bite at the café. Can I treat you to something?"

"That would be awesome, Tom. Then maybe you could give me an idea of where I could get some work. I need to get a job so we can afford an apartment."

Tom surprised himself by enjoying the visit with Allen and Charlene. Baby Jasmine was asleep, and they talked for an hour about their younger days. Charlene was interested, so both men avoided any reference to the hard times. Tom suggested a few places in town that might have some work for Allen and although he didn't mention it, he thought of the project at the Lodge. Maybe he would ask Peyton if there was room in the budget to hire another employee. Working with Allen would give him a chance to see if he had changed his life. He hoped that Allen meant what he said. Their mother had been through a lot in her life, and he didn't want Allen to open old wounds. He would drive him away if he did anything to hurt Helen again.

After lunch in the local diner, a few of the regulars dropped by their table to welcome Allen back and get introduced to his wife. Baby Jasmine entertained with dimple smiles and wriggling arms. Tom chatted with Charlene and learned that she grew up in Montana, and her parents moved their family into Canada when Charlene was a teenager. She had an older sister and two younger brothers who were all living in Calgary. Charlene and Allen had met at the annual Calgary Stampede and had been living together for two years now.

Tom looked at his watch. "I'd love to chat more folks, but I really need to get back to work. It's been great, meeting with you! Let's do this again soon." The baby was getting fussy anyway and needed an afternoon nap. They exchanged cell phone numbers, and Tom promised to call Allen if he had any leads. Outside, Tom touched Allen's arm and pulled him back for a moment. "I'm very glad you're back, Al, and I'm happy for you, but I sure hope this is for real. I don't want you to hurt Mom again. Every time you came home high and then disappeared again, she got so depressed. She loves you and your new family, and I want her to be with them with no problems."

"I'm sorry, man." Allen put a hand on Tom's shoulder. "Listen, I spent a lot of time this past year in recovery and I'm clean now. I've turned over a new leaf, with help from the Lord and from Charlene. She means everything to me now. Having a fiancé and baby has made me realize what a mess I made of my life. All I want now is to get a job to support my family and gain your trust. Charlene and I aren't officially married yet, but we want to tie the knot when we've saved enough to make it a lovely event."

Tom hugged his brother. "Keep in touch and let me know how the job hunt goes. And take good care of your sweet girls."

On his way home that afternoon, Tom stopped at the Lodge to see how things were coming along and found Peyton sweeping up gyp-roc and sawdust for the dumpster. "Where is everybody? Done for the day?"

Peyton warmed him with her smile. "Slow day today… the delivery truck had a breakdown and won't be here until tomorrow, and the guys have been working hard all day, so I sent them home early. How are things at your place?"

Tom sighed as he poured himself a coffee. "Okay, although it's been quite a day."

"Trouble on your site?" She was intrigued with the idea of log homes and could imagine how hard the work would be. He looked exhausted.

Tom hesitated, wondering if he should share family matters. He hardly knew Peyton but had seen how much she cared about her family. Now she seemed willing to share his. "My long-lost brother turned up at the worksite today. I haven't seen hide nor hair of him for over a year."

"Wow! Isn't that a good thing?" As an only child, she

had often wished for a brother or sister. But judging from his expression, it wasn't the same for Tom.

"I'm not sure." Tom grabbed a folding chair and straddled it. "Allen has been in and out of trouble for the past few years, moving from place to place, getting himself into difficult situations and needing us to bail him out. Whenever he did show up at home, it was to ask for money. We could tell he was involved with drugs, and we feared gangs as well. It was so hard on Mom that I finally told him not to come home until he cleaned up his life."

"So now he's back. How does he seem to you?"

Tom rubbed his face with both hands and looked over at her. "I don't honestly know. He looks good! He has a fiancé now and a daughter. He says he's clean and sober, and they plan to stay here and get jobs."

"Tom! That's wonderful. Just think…he's the prodigal son returning. And you're an uncle!"

"Yeah, well I'm not so sure about it. He has let us down so many times before. I'm thinking about my mother, and the times Allen would disappear for days, sometimes weeks. Numerous times we went out looking for him, wondering if he was passed out in an alley, or living in a tent city, worrying that he had overdosed. Sometimes Mom would cry for days, thinking he might be dead. Not knowing…until we got a knock at the door and there he'd be. Always with excuses about working but being fired, or someone stole his money. Mom would insist he stay for a few days so we could help him out, and she gave him money, but he would be gone the next day." The bitterness welled up in his throat. "I hate the idea of going through that again. And I don't know if Mom could take it anymore."

"Oh, Tom." Peyton touched his arm gently. "I'm sorry

for what you've gone through with him. But everyone should have a second chance for a better life. Perhaps now that he has a family, he is truly repentant for what he's done. God loves Allen and He brought him back into your life for a reason, Tom. He needs a brother right now, especially one like you, to support and encourage, and be a role model for him. Think about his fiancé and baby… they need your help too. A family is everything and you need each other."

Tom sighed. "You're right. But it's going to be awfully hard. With all the baggage he's carrying, I'm having trouble trusting him." He looked up at her and his face softened. "An uncle, eh? That's something. A responsibility I'm going to take on. For the sake of that sweet baby." He smiled at Peyton. "Thanks for your support, Peyton. I appreciate all you are doing for everyone." Suddenly he reached out his arms and folded her in them. "You are a good friend." For a second, they stood together and Tom looked into her eyes. Then she pushed away from him. She couldn't let her heart stand in the way of their duties at the Lodge. Only a few more weeks and the place would be put up for sale. She would be heading home.

TEN

T om left shortly after, saying he had to go home to take Carver to the vet, and Peyton finished her clean-up. The delivery truck never showed up when it was supposed to, and when she got a call that it wasn't coming until the next day, she decided she was tired and wouldn't mind a bit of time for herself. She headed out to the motorhome to shower and change. She would enjoy a jaunt into town and supper at the diner. She felt conspicuous driving the big rig but so what? It was all she had.

She kept thinking of her last call with Dave. He had sounded stronger and itching to get mobile again. "I'm glad to be home and looking after myself now." Happily, their church had been there for him, even though he and Peyton had not been active members since his wife's death. She would be ever grateful to Ellie Mitchell and Pastor Bob, who gladly offered to take some responsibility for him, and for the ladies' auxiliary who were making sure he got a hot meal every day. Having a home care nurse look in on him frequently and someone else doing a bit of housekeeping until he felt able, he would be fine. She smiled to herself. Dave was probably enjoying the women coming to visit.

Talking with her dad and realizing how good the church members were to him, gave Peyton a lump in her throat. These same folks had rallied around them when her mother was dying of cancer a couple of years ago. Peyton had stopped attending church to look after her mother, though, and had lost touch with her own friends. She had prayed so hard for her mother to be healed! But when she got more and more ill, something in Peyton began to shut down. Where was the God she was pleading to? It seemed that He had closed his ears to her passionate pleas. And when her mother breathed her last, Peyton vowed never to go back to church again.

Now, she gave herself a mental shake. This was supposed to be a restful afternoon. That was the past and there was nothing to be gained by bringing it up again. She was grateful to those good people who were back in Dave's life, but she felt a twinge of guilt for not being with him herself. What must they think, her not being at her dad's bedside? Maybe they didn't realize that Dave had insisted she stay to complete the project. If she had folded on him, they would lose a lot of money and maybe even their company.

Dave had asked about Tom and how things were working out for her. She assured him that Tom was a hard worker and she appreciated having him working alongside her. Dave was glad. "I can tell he is a decent, honest man, and a man of faith. I'm thankful that he is the one working for us. us." Peyton felt the same and knew that her father was a good judge of character. If her dad trusted Tom, she would too. She would do her utmost to make this flip the finest one they'd ever done. That was the best thing she could do to help her dad heal.

She did a few errands in town and then headed for the diner where she and Julie had lunched a couple of weeks before. It was small with a somewhat limited menu, but the owner was very friendly and the food was delicious, at least the meal she and Julie had enjoyed previously. She would try another item on the menu today.

"Come on in, honey," the waitress called to her. "Sit wherever you like." Peyton was surprised to see Tom at a booth with a brunette. They looked like they were enjoying themselves. He caught her eye and stood up with a wide smile. "Hello! Come and join us!" Peyton wanted to refuse, but it was too late. The brunette narrowed her eyes at her, and quickly moved around the booth so she could sit with Tom, not Peyton. Tom was a bit flustered but remained a gentleman, introducing the women to each another, and waving to the waitress to take her order.

"Tom and I were high school sweethearts, weren't we, sweetie?" Tracey leaned over against Tom and smiled coyly at him. "Now we're rekindling an old flame, aren't we, Tom?"

Tom cleared his throat. "I wouldn't say that." His eyes met Peyton's. "Just helping a friend who needs a hand up." He changed the subject quickly. "Peyton is new in town. She and her dad are renovating the Lodge."

"Really? I can't imagine why. No one would want to live there. Too spooky!"

"My father and I choose to update it and make it a beautiful hotel again. It will take us about three months and then it will be for sale."

"Peyton is a journeyman carpenter," Tom piped in. "From the city."

"How nice for you," Tracey drawled, clearly disinterested. "I'm a city girl too. Can't wait to get back there."

Peyton tried to be polite. "I like Calgary...I know it well. I've lived there all my life. The Rockies are so beautiful though. I'd love to live here permanently, but our home and business are based in the city. How about you, Tracey? Are you just visiting here?"

Tracey reached over, put her hand over Tom's and looked up at him. "I'm not sure. Depends how things go. Doesn't it, Tom?"

Peyton suddenly realized the others had finished their meals and the waitress was taking away their plates. She had no desire to sit and eat in front of Tom's girlfriend. "Could you please box this for me? I have another errand to do, so would you excuse me?" Tom was surprised. She smiled at them and stood up to leave. "Nice to meet you, Tracey. Bye, Tom." She didn't wait for a reply. Tracey smirked but said nothing.

Out in the motorhome, Peyton wondered why she was feeling so flustered. She and Tom had a business relationship only, and that should be clearly defined. But she felt a pang of annoyance at the thought of Tom and Tracey together. She was clearly staking her claim to Tom and wanted to make sure Peyton knew it. She wondered what Tom had seen in the girl when they were high school sweethearts. Not that she should care. In a few weeks the renovations would be done and she would be back in the city with her dad. She must not let herself get attached to anything - not the mountains, the Lodge or Tom.

After Peyton left, Tom moved across the table from Tracey to discuss the reason they were having lunch together. Tom had connected her with Andre at the motel, but he felt responsible to make sure she didn't abuse the favor.

"What's happening at the motel now, Tracey? What are your plans? You have that room free for a week, but you can't stay there forever. What's happening in your life?"

She sighed. "I'm in trouble, Tom. Here's the thing. I used

to have a substantial trust fund from my grandparents that was created for me when I was a child. It was set up so that when I reached the age of twenty, I became my own trustee and was able to withdraw money whenever wanted to. I did just that for a while and loved it. My parents were never home, and my friends and I partied a lot around the country and I bought whatever I wanted. When I got tired of that, I met Barrett again and we got married. He wanted to start a family right away but I never wanted kids. I was an only child and liked the idea. I was having too much fun on my own. He didn't know it, but I used birth control for a few years, and when he found out, he was outraged. Our marriage started to go to pieces."

Tracey had hardly touched her lunch and let the waitress take her plate away. She looked at Tom and saw he meant business. "There's more. Barrett and I broke up because I was having an affair with someone else. We divorced and he moved out, and I put our condo up for sale. When it sold, Barrett gave me half of the money and I moved in with my lover. Three months later, I discovered that he had found how to access my bank account and cleared it out! He took off, leaving me to pay the rent, which I couldn't do. I went to my parents for money to tide me over for a few months." She paused, eyes filling and lips trembling. "My father said no. He had bailed me out of too many things in the past and wouldn't do it anymore."

Tom didn't want to know what the other situations were. He was glad that he hadn't married Tracey after they graduated high school, like she wanted back then. Nevertheless, he felt a pang of sympathy for her now. "What about Barrett? Is he with someone else?"

"I have no idea." She was tearful. "And in any case, I would never ask him to take me back." She looked up at

Tom. "I really hurt him when I was unfaithful, and after being in other relationships, I realize now what a good husband he was."

Tom was appalled but tried not to show it. "I guess the time has come for you to grow up, Tracey. You're on your own now. There are lots of possibilities of getting a job somewhere. You could apply at fast-food places. Ask Andre if he needs more chambermaids. There's an employment office here in town too, that might help you find something."

Tracy looked up at him and angrily wiped the tears away. "Chambermaid? No way! And I could never work at some hamburger joint. Can't you give me a hand up like you said? Or was that just to impress your girlfriend?"

"She's not my girlfriend. And don't change the subject. You need to start thinking about your future, Tracey. It's time for you to stand on your own two feet."

Without a word, Tracy grabbed her handbag and stomped out of the diner. The waitress came to the table. "You're smart to stay clear of that girl. She's been nothing but trouble since she came to town."

ELEVEN

Becoming an uncle was something that changed Tom's perspective completely. After giving it a lot of consideration, he decided he would put Allen to the test and see just how committed he was to his new lifestyle. If Allen did what he pledged - remain clean and sober, Tom vowed to do whatever he could to help him. If Allen failed, which in Tom's mind was certainly a possibility, he would fill the gap and make sure Charlene and the baby were provided for. Either way, Tom was going to keep an eye on Allen and make sure the vulnerable members of his family were protected.

Tom's first thought was to approach Peyton about hiring Allen. "I don't think he has much experience but I will work with him to make sure he does things right." Peyton agreed readily, pleased to be able to help them both. Since she didn't have siblings herself, she was moved at the opportunity to help unite the two brothers. Tom asked her to bring Allen to the job site to meet her. They arranged a time for that afternoon and at Peyton's insistence, Allen brought his family too so she could meet them.

After introducing Allen and Charlene to Peyton, Tom gave Allen a tour of the Lodge, pointing out what still needed to be done. Allen was an eager listener, realizing that working on a project like this would give him some valuable work experience for the future. It was love at first sight for Peyton and Jasmine, as it had been for Tom. Charlene was shy but Peyton drew her out by talking about baby things as women do.

Peyton confirmed that she would be happy to hire Allen, and they discussed the time and wages that he could expect. Allen gave her their contact information, and it was agreed that he would start work the next morning.

Both young people were thankful as they left. Peyton was pleased about the meeting too. "Charlene is lovely and seems to be a good mom. Allen seems quite sincere about making a new start here. I think he will do well."

"Let's hope so. I want him to work alongside of me for a while." Tom remembered Allen's whispered words at the door: "Thanks for having faith in me, Al. I won't let you down."

Later that evening, Tom was leaving work, planning to go home and change for a promised dinner at his mother's apartment. He decided to give her a call to see if there was anything he could bring. "Yes, you can bring that nice young lady you're always talking about. I'd like to meet her." Tom chuckled. "Peyton, my mom wants to know if you would like to come to supper at her place. Roast beef with all the trimmings!"

It was on Peyton's lips to make an excuse but the prospect of a home-cooked dinner was too much to resist. "I'd like that very much. Thank you!" Both Tom and Helen were pleased. "We'll be there shortly, Mom. See you soon!"

Peyton locked up the Lodge and went to the motorhome, and Tom was to pick her up in half an hour.

Right on time, Peyton was waiting at the gate when his truck pulled up.

"Wow! You sure cleaned up nice," he exclaimed, admiring her pretty dress and up-swept hair-do. Just a touch of make-up suited him fine. He hated the look of women who plastered on foundation and drew heavy eyebrows. He was glad to see that Peyton was wholesome looking, with a more natural look. He had changed into blue jeans and a long-sleeve plaid shirt, with shiny cowboy boots on his feet. "You're looking pretty good yourself," Peyton responded. "All you need is a cowboy hat." He pointed over his shoulder to the back seat. "Probably some dog hair on it, but that's okay."

Peyton climbed into the truck and Tom backed out of the yard. "What kind of dog do you have?" She loved animals. "I'd love to meet him."

"Golden Retriever. You haven't seen Carver yet? We'll have to do something about that. He's my best buddy and loves everybody. Not much of a watch dog for that reason, although he's scared away a bear or two in his day and has the scars to prove it. I'll introduce him to you sometime. I'll take you to see my pigmy goats too. They're cute little things. Carver is their protector."

"That's sweet! I'd love to see them. We never had a pet when I was growing up, except for a yellow canary that my mom loved. He sang his heart out every day. But when my mom got cancer and passed away, the bird never sang again. We found him dead in the cage. I don't know if it was a coincidence or if he died because he missed her."

"How long ago did your mom pass away?"

"It will be four years in September. And I still think of her every day."

Tom knew how it felt to lose a parent but his was for a different reason. His dad just disappeared without any explanation when he was a kid. Sometimes he thought it would have been better if his dad had died. At least the family would have known what happened and had some closure.

"Tell me more about your mom, Tom. I'm getting a bit nervous about meeting her."

"No worries, she's going to love you. Her name is Helen McCauley and she lives in an apartment above a convenience store. Mom started working there when she was in high school, and still does. The owner, Mr. Fox, was a nice old gentleman with no family of his own, so he really liked us kids and encouraged Mom to bring us to his store. When Dad left us, we had to move from our home to a smaller place, because Mom was struggling financially. Mr. Fox knew that, and he would give us treats and things, and even send Mom home with whole bags of groceries to tide her over. He would tell her the items were outdated or weren't selling, and he wanted to get rid of them. We knew differently. He loved Mom like a daughter and when he died, he left the building and the store to her in his will, and a significant amount of money for ongoing maintenance. Mom moved us from an old house we were living in, to the apartment above the store, and she's lived there ever since."

"What a story! He must have really loved you all to be so generous."

"Yes, he was like a grandpa to us, and we were all sad when he passed away. He was a great guy." Tom chuckled at a memory. "Allen was only three or four, I think, when we first started going with Mom to the store. Mr. Fox was funny looking to us kids. He wore these little round glasses that made his eyes look huge. The first time Allen saw him, he was terrified. Wouldn't go near the man, and it took quite a while for him to get over it. It hurt the old man's feelings a bit, but eventually they became pals. He loved us all and we really missed him when he died."

"So did your mom hire someone else to help with the store?"

"Nope! At least not at first. She put us kids to work, and that was the only job I had until I graduated high school and went off to trade school. Allen helped for a while when I went away but then he started acting weird and taking off with his friends, and Mom couldn't count on him to be home. Eventually she hired Esther to ensure someone was always there. You'll meet her on our way in. She's Mom's best friend and has been working here for years."

"Your mother must be an amazing woman. I can't wait to meet her!"

"Well, we're here!" Tom pulled into a small parking lot beside a red brick building. "She's excited to meet you too, and she's a great cook, so I'm sure you'll enjoy yourself."

Tom took Peyton through the store to the back stairway, greeting customers and receiving a friendly hug from Esther. "How are you, Tom? Nice to see you. Whatever your Mom is cooking upstairs smells wonderful!"

"We'll be sure to save some for you. This is my friend Peyton. She's in charge of the Lodge renovations everyone has been talking about."

"Well, good for you! Tom has told me about it. The town is excited about having it open again after all these years. When do you expect it to be finished?"

"Not sure but everything is going well, so we're optimistic. You're not on your own this evening, are you?"

"Just for now, but my grandson should be here any minute to help until closing. He's on the high school football team so I'm sure he'll keep me safe. Enjoy your evening!"

Peyton was impressed with the charming little store that was clean and bright, with a surprising variety of items, "from soup to nuts" as her mother would have said. She smiled at customers as they walked to the back and a few called hellos to Tom. As well as the usual groceries and other items, Peyton noticed displays of beautiful handmade crafts for sale on consignment. A nice way for neighborhood artists to display their work. The area looked pleasant but, in the back Peyton noticed a heavily barred door and an alarm system on the wall beside it. No matter how nice the neighborhood was, it was a good idea to play it safe.

A door opened at the top of the staircase and Helen appeared. Tom ushered Peyton to go ahead of him up the steps. At the top, an elderly lady with a wide smile and sparkling eyes was holding a little black dog. ""Welcome, Peyton dear! So nice to have you. Tom has been praising about you for some time now."

Peyton blushed and reached out to scratch the puppy's ears and was rewarded with licks. She looked over at Tom. "He's been saying the same about you, Mrs. McCauley. Thank you so much for inviting me."

"Please call me Helen. And you come here, big guy! Give your mom a hug. It's high time you came for a visit."

"Mom, I was here last Sunday."

"I know, but I never get tired of having you. Come in and shut the door, honey. We don't want Barkley to run down into the store. Hope you like dogs, Peyton. Barkley loves everybody and isn't shy about it. How was your day, Tom?"

"Fine, Mom. I brought you a few things but they're still down in the truck. I'll bring them up before we go. Anything we can do to help?"

"Thanks, but no need. Everything's under control. Dinner's almost ready."

Peyton took a seat and her lap was immediately filled with the little dog. "Aren't you a pretty boy," she crooned. "What kind of dog is Barkley, Helen?"

"Shih Zu cross with Bichon. He's not a puppy now... he's about six years old, we think. We adopted him from the local SPCA." Helen looked at him fondly. "He's the fourth Shih Tzu our family has had. The other three we raised from birth, but they've been put down over the years for various health reasons. This little guy is a real sweetheart."

Expecting the apartment to be small and crowded, Peyton was surprised at how large and beautiful it was. Helen was pleased. "Tom and his friends did some renovations for me a couple of years ago. He's so talented. I'm proud of him."

"This is absolutely stunning! Everything bright and airy, and so coordinated! It's like something from a magazine. I see you have one of those tube skylights. They're great! My friend has one too, in her dining room. It cuts down on the power bill too."

"Would you like to see the rest of the place? I'm sure Tom would be glad to show you around. I need to finish a few things in the kitchen. Why don't you and Barkley give her a little tour?"

Tom described what the building had been like previously and the changes they had made. It had been renovated so that the whole top floor of the building was Helen's apartment. The main area was open plan with beautiful oak floors, a contemporary kitchen, and a living room with a gas fireplace and a large picture window. Tom and his crew had updated the master bedroom and added an ensuite bathroom. The main bathroom, and the other bedrooms where Tom and Allen used to sleep, had been painted and spruced up. One was now Helen's office and sewing room, and the other had a double bed and dresser saved for guests. The décor everywhere showed Helen's good taste.

Back at the dining area, Peyton expressed her admiration. "You've done a wonderful job, folks. This apartment could rival anything I've seen in the city. And what a lovely view!" The picture window framed the nearby Rocky Mountains.

"Yes, I'm very proud of it all, and those who made it possible. I'm happy to share it with you. Please come now and we'll eat."

After having so many meals eaten in her motorhome over the last weeks, Peyton didn't have to be asked twice. Helen had cooked a succulent beef roast with all the trimmings, including Yorkshire Pudding, Peyton's favorite. The meal was fantastic. Between bites, Helen kept the conversation going, interested in knowing more about Peyton and her dad, the schooling she took to get her journeyman ticket, and the work she and Tom were doing on the Lodge. It felt good to be dining across from Tom in such a lovely place. It was ages since she'd enjoyed the company of others like this. At home, she and her dad ate out a lot, and when they did cook something, it was a frozen meal in front of the TV watching the news. Helen was delightful to be with, as she chatted with her guests and got Tom talking about his work as a log home builder. Seeing Tom in this setting showed Peyton a lot about him. She had heard it said that if you want to see the measure of a man, watch how he treats his mother. It was clear that Tom loved and respected his mother, and that she was very proud of him.

Frequently Peyton and Tom exchanged glances and

smiles across the table and when they did, Peyton felt a stirring inside. He was a special man, she could see that, and one that any woman would want for a husband. Too bad he was in a relationship with Tracey, who had so obviously laid claim to him in the restaurant. She didn't seem to be Tom's type, though. And why wasn't Tracey here having supper with Helen instead of Peyton? She wondered just how strong a hold Tracey had with Tom. Far be it from her to come between them. No matter, Peyton and her dad would soon be finished the Lodge flip and on their way back to city life.

Over coffee and dessert in the comfort of the living room, Helen brought up the topic of Allen. "Tom tells me that you've given him a job, Peyton. Thank you so much for doing that. He really needs the work. Have you met his wife and baby?"

Peyton glanced over at Tom, who had leaned back in his chair with crossed arms. "Yes, I have met them. They seem very nice and Jasmine is adorable."

"Yes, isn't she? I'm so happy to be a grandma!" Helen looked over at Tom and sighed. "Allen has somewhat of a checkered past but underneath it all he's a good boy."

Tom cleared his throat and took a swig of coffee. "Checkered is putting it mildly."

"Allen was a difficult child to raise, I have to admit, especially in his teen years. He was willful, careless, looking for fun in all the wrong places. Allen was ten years old and Tom fourteen when our family splintered." She shook her head sadly and laid a hand on Tom's arm. "Tom carried that burden nobly and was my strength, and the man of the family, during those trying times. And he still takes good care of me. But Allen?" She shook her head. "He's brought both Tom and I a lot of sorrow over the years. We've coped with it the best we can, and in spite of everything, I still love him. God does too." She paused. "I must say, I was shocked when he turned up this time with a family. I didn't know what to think at first. But we had a long talk and I watched him with Charlene and the baby. He loves them, and I believe he has a sincere intention to turn his life around. It's a big responsibility to have a wife and child, and I think he deserves our support. I've been praying that this time Allen will succeed."

"Thank you for your honesty, Mrs. McCauley." Peyton leaned forward and took Helen's hand. "I am willing to help Allen as much as I can. Tom has assured me that he will be there to keep him focused and help him to develop some skills. Our current flip has a three-month time frame and we've already used up quite a bit of that. There is some steady work for him now as we head toward completion, but soon the Lodge will be up for sale, and I'll be packing up and heading back to Calgary. Our company is based there. This is the first time we've done a flip so far away from home, and it probably won't happen again. With my father's condition, I can't promise any work past this. But I'm happy to have Allen on board now and we'll help him do a good job."

"Thank you, Peyton." Helen reached up to brush tears from her eyes. "That's all we can ask for. Tom told me about your dad's accident. I'm so sorry! I'll pray that he gets well soon." She straightened up, touched her nose with a tissue and squared her shoulders. "Have you seen where Allen and Charlene are staying?"

Tom frowned. "Last I heard from Allen, they were living at the Timberland Hotel."

"They were there when they first came to town, but Allen told me that a friend of his is letting them stay in his trailer right now." Helen sighed. "I drove by there the other day and saw Charlene coming out of it. It's parked in the lot of Brewster's Pub."

"Really?" Both Tom and Peyton were shocked. "Not the best place for a recovering addict to be living."

"That's what I thought too." Helen shook her head. "I stopped and talked with her. The trailer is very small and she has it tidy and clean, but when I asked her about the amenities, she was embarrassed. They have make-shift power and water hook-ups but no proper bathroom facilities. They're using the bathrooms in the pub when it's open but there are no showers or bathtubs, of course. I think it's terrible. She has a baby that needs proper care. I hate the thought of them having to live there." Helen turned in her chair and looked Tom straight in the eye. "You can do something to help them, Tom. If you are willing."

Tom changed his position and propped his head on one arm. "Awe, Mom…we've talked about this before. I don't want Allen living with me."

Helen looked at him sternly. "I offered Allen and Charlene the rooms here with me but they declined. Not private enough, I guess, and they didn't want to disturb me with the baby and all. I would have loved it though. But you, Tom, have a beautiful home with a lovely suite in the basement. Sitting empty for how many years? It would be perfect for your brother and his family. You would be giving Allen an amazing hand up if you let him live in that apartment."

Tom got up and paced in front of the fireplace. "I let him stay there once before, Mom, and I don't know if I can trust him. What if he falls off the wagon? Have you forgotten what his drugged friends did back then? Remember the meth lab they created down there? It cost me a lot of money and time to clean up the mess he left behind. Not to mention dealing with the police. We haven't seen Allen for over a year. We don't know what he's been doing, or what his friends are like now."

"That was then. Things are different now. It's your house. Keep an eye on him and if you see some activity you don't approve of, stop him in his tracks. But give him a chance, Tom. He says he's a new man. If after a few weeks or months his lifestyle changes to something you're not comfortable with, you can kick him out. I don't think that would happen, but there wouldn't be a hassle if you had to evict people like last time. Right now, think of his lovely fiancé and baby. Don't they deserve a better place to live?"

Tom had no answer and turned away to lean against the mantle. There was an uncomfortable few moments and Helen got up and began to stack plates. "Tommy, remember the Bible story about the Prodigal Son? We need to welcome our prodigal home, no matter what he's done. He's your brother…he's family. He wouldn't have come back here if he didn't need our help, and our love. I believe this time it will be better. I've been told that he's coming back to church and there are people there who will support him in many ways, not just us. If others are willing, shouldn't his own family be doing all they can?

Tom sighed, resting his head against the mantle, then turned and looked ruefully at Peyton. "She's a hard sell, isn't she? Mom, I don't want to be the petty older brother in the story He smiled down at her. "I'll talk to Allen in the morning."

Helen's eyes were wet as she came to hug him and Peyton felt her own eyes fill. To give them a private moment, she picked up some dishes and took them to the kitchen. When she turned back, Tom was behind her and on impulse she gave his arm a squeeze. "You're a good guy," she whispered. "I'm so glad to know you and your family." He met her eyes and for a moment she thought he was going to kiss her. She smiled and turned away, wondering if he was thinking the same. *What would it be like to be part of his family, the love of his life? Sadly, she would never know. She and Dave were only there to do a flip. As soon as the renovations were completed, they would go back to the city. That thought made her very sad.*

TWELVE

The next morning, Peyton had a hard time getting motivated. She hardly slept and was feeling the results. Coming home from the lovely dinner at Helen's, Tom and Peyton had barely spoken. They had stayed to help Helen clean up the kitchen and Tom found a hockey game to watch, but he seemed restless, so as soon as everything was done, they had bid farewell. Both were tired from the day's work and stuffed from dinner, but it was more than that. Peyton wondered if Tom was having second thoughts about that moment of connection that seemed to fan a flame. When he dropped her off at the motorhome, she wished he would kiss her goodnight, yet she was relieved when he didn't. It would have changed their working relationship completely, and she didn't want to do anything to make the flip any harder than it already was. She had a lot of responsibility and she couldn't take a chance of her employees seeing it.

After a strong coffee she felt better and left the motorhome just in time to see Allen coming up the driveway. He was early, which was a good sign for his first day of work. He gave her a wide smile and a handshake, thanking her again for giving him the job. Peyton unlocked the Lodge doors and they went inside, with Peyton wondering where Tom was. He was usually there by now and had said he would be sure to be there to greet Allen.

Moments later Tom arrived, carrying a tray of coffee and a box of donut holes. "Got French Vanilla coffee for you," he whispered to Peyton. "Thought you might like it." She accepted it and a handful of donut holes with thanks, then discreetly moved away. As Tom passed a cup to Allen, he nodded toward a table in the corner. "Let's sit for a few minutes, Bro. We need to chat."

After a bit of small talk about the job site, and making sure Allen had the safety gear he needed for the day, Tom cleared his throat. "Before we start our day, I've got a proposition for you. How would you and Charlene like to move into my basement suite?"

Allen looked at him in amazement, and then blurted, "We already have a place to stay."

"Yes, I know. I went by there this morning." Tom's voice was gentle. "Did Charlene tell you that she had a visit from Mom yesterday?"

A shadow came across Allen's face. "Yes, she did. I know Mom would like us to have a better place to live, and that's my intention once I get steady work."

"Mom told me that Charlene was doing a good job keeping the trailer clean and neat, but it really is too small for the three of you. I'm sure you would prefer something else, but the rental market in this town is expensive, and what is available right now isn't fit for a family. Mom and I would like you to have something more suitable."

"I don't need your charity, Tom." Allen's face was flushed and stony. "I can look after my own family. I just need a few good pay checks and we'll be okay."

"Look, man…I was dumbfounded when you came back here with Charlene and Jasmine. Never thought I'd be an uncle at my age. But after seeing you guys, I think it's wonderful. I'd like to help you out, now that you're a family man. It must be hard for you to take care of them in the trailer. You need a proper home. My basement suite has been sitting empty for a long time and I haven't rented it out because I didn't want just anyone living there. Having you folks stay there will help me too, knowing someone I trust is looking after it. What do you think?"

Allen sighed. "Do you trust me? After all the things that happened at your place the last time I was there?"

"That's in the past, Allen. You've told me those days are long gone, and I'm willing to forget them if you're willing to accept this offer."

"Not without giving you some rent money."

"Of course! But not right away. When you've been working for a few months, and get on your feet, we can discuss that issue. But right now, everything is there for you...heat, power, cable and even a bit of furniture. What do you say?"

Allen looked down at his hands for a moment, and then up at Tom with moist eyes. "After all the heartache I've caused you and Mom over the years, I'm surprised you would even consider letting me live there."

"Well, that was in the past. I know you're a different man now and you won't let me down. I'm willing to take that chance."

"Thank you." Allen's face lit up and he met Tom's eyes with a smile. "Charlene will be thrilled."

Tom smiled and put his hand over Allen's. "Give me a day or two to get some stuff cleaned out and then we'll help you move in. I haven't been downstairs for a while. I think there's some furniture left by a previous tenant. Mom says she has kitchen stuff if you need it. And there's a Salvation Army Thrift Store in town that I go to all the time. We can check it out for other things you need." Tom paused and grinned. "That's settled then, Ally", using the nickname of their youth. "I'm really glad you're back."

Peyton hadn't heard the conversation but saw the two men stand and embrace. Tom met her eyes and gave her a thumbs up. The man was always known for helping others and now he was making a way for his long-lost brother to care for his family. She smiled at the warmth of his gaze. He was without a doubt, a man with a heart.

Allen wasn't the only new hire that morning. They heard a vehicle in the driveway and in came Jason, the teenager who would be doing community hours. Tom welcomed him warmly and introduced him to Peyton and the crew as a "volunteer". Jason would come every weekday morning to work outside, looking after the gardens and doing any other chores as needed. His mom would pick him up in time for his afternoon classes. Jason appeared a bit sullen at first but perked up once she had gone. His first chore would be cutting the grass with the lawn tractor, which Tom knew he would love to do. It was obvious that he liked and respected Tom, and he started the job eagerly.

Peyton had in mind what she wanted accomplished that day and it turned out to be one of the most productive mornings she had since the project started. More building materials and plumbing fixtures had arrived the day before and local plumbers were on site, beginning their hard tasks. Tom had brought a few of his men from his Pioneer Log Homes site to help the project get caught up to schedule. With saws running, hammers banging and supplies getting carted back and forth up and down, it truly was a busy day. Tom took over monitoring Allen and Jason, who seemed to be getting along well with each other.

When Peyton took a break, she looked around at all the activity and her spirits lifted. With this crew, thanks to Tom, they had a good chance to make their three-month timeframe after all. Dave would be pleased. He was determined to take the trip to the site himself as soon as his doctor released him. She gave him a call and they did an online walk-about. The Lodge had a small elevator so he would be able to get around easily. The stairs to the loft were a bit steep but he could deal with that when the time came. Perhaps with a couple of strong men to help, he could be assisted up. The more Dave talked about it, the more she longed to see him. She missed him so much and wanted to show him all that had been accomplished so far.

Just then, there was a knock at the door and in walked the ladies - Julie, Helen and Charlene with Jasmine. Surprise!" Tom and Allen appeared and there were hugs all around.

Julie looked around the area in wonder. "You're doing some amazing things with this place, Peyton. I'm very impressed!"

"Thanks, Julie. Still quite a bit to do, as you can see, but we're getting there."

Peyton captured Jasmine's tiny hand and got a smile in return. "I didn't realize you knew each other, although I should have expected it in a small town."

"Yes, Helen and I are good friends. I went to school with Tom, although I was a grade ahead. We all go to the same church too, and that's why we're here. Our ladies' group has donated some money to buy Jasmine a crib and other baby stuff, to help Allen and Charlene get on their feet. We're on our way to the city."

Tom grinned. "What? You can't buy a crib here?"

Helen slapped his arm. "Of course! But there will be

a better selection in city stores, and us gals deserve a break anyway."

Hellen caught Peyton's arm and drew her aside while the ladies looked around the ground floor. "It's a long way, but we're planning to stay a couple of days. Would you like to come with us? It would give you break from everything, and we thought it would be nice to get to know each other better, have some fun and you could spend some time with your dad."

Peyton's face lit up at the possibility but then faded. "There is still so much to do here, though. We've been using Tom and his team a lot to help, and I really shouldn't take the time."

Tom stepped up and put a gentle hand on her arm. "Don't worry about that, Peyton. We've done a lot of work already. I can look after things until you get back."

"That would be wonderful. I've been thinking about him so much these last few days. I really would like to see for myself how he's doing."

"Please come, Peyton!" Helen clapped her hands and hugged Peyton. "It'll be so much fun. I know this is short notice, but we can wait while you get your things together."

"Are you sure you don't mind?" Peyton turned to Tom. "I don't want to louse up things at your site."

Tom smiled down at her and she saw a warmth in his eyes that made her catch a breath. "Go honey," he whispered. "You deserve it. I'll look after these folks while you get ready."

Within minutes Peyton had cleaned up, packed a bag and was ready to go. The others had gone out to the back yard, and Tom was sitting in a chair bouncing Jasmine on his knee. "It will be good to go home and get some more clothes. I'm tired of wearing the same things for six weeks."

"You look beautiful in whatever you wear." Tom surprised himself and felt his face grow warm. He reached into a pocket and pulled out some cash, pressing it into her hand. He gave her a shy smile. "Put this toward whatever Jasmine needs."

"Something special from Uncle Tom?" she teased. She loved his obvious attachment to Jasmine. He would make a wonderful daddy for someone, someday.

Soon the ladies were on their way in Julie's car, Peyton in front, and Helen and Charlene in the back with Jasmine's car seat between them. "So glad you could come, Peyton," Helen said, squeezing her shoulder. "I really enjoyed your company the other day. My son admires you very much, you know. We all think you're so brave to do what you're doing, and we can see that Tom admires much more than your abilities on the job site."

The other ladies chuckled. "I could see it in his eyes the day he first met you," Julie chimed in. "We agreed then that he was very handsome, didn't we? And now he definitely has his eyes set on you."

"Oh, I don't think so," Peyton protested, feeling her face growing warm. "We have a business relationship, that's all. He's been a great help and I really appreciate it. If all goes well, the Lodge will be finished soon and we'll put it up for sale. I'll be going home to the city." Even as she said it, she felt a pang of sadness. "I'll be sorry to go, though."

"Long distance romances rarely work out, take it from me." Helen smiled sadly. "I had a beau years ago when I was young. We had a lot of trouble scheduling our romance. He was a very handsome too, and we had feelings for each other, but he was a train engineer, always away when I wanted him. Eventually we just had to call it quits." She paused at the memory, and then smiled brightly at Peyton. "But I know the answer for you. You'll just have to stay here!"

Everyone laughed and Peyton smiled. "Nice thought but probably not." The other ladies went on to another topic and she let her mind wander. *Could I actually do that? Do I really want to go back home, to the house I grew up in, sharing with my dad? I treasure so many memories of Mom there, but maybe it's time for me to let go. I should be out on my own, in my own place. I'm 25 years old and should be independent. But I couldn't leave Dad on his own, with his injury and the company business. Will things ever be the same? Or do I even want them to?*

Arriving in the city, the ladies spent the rest of the afternoon at a mall where they bought a beautiful crib for Jasmine, the kind that could be made into a single bed when she was old enough. The church donation was substantial and Tom topped the amount so they could afford to buy sheets and blankets as well. Charlene and the ladies had fun picking out what she needed for the baby in the way of everyday clothing, as well as a few little dresses they couldn't resist. Each of the ladies wanted to give on their own, so by the time they were finished shopping, the trunk of the car was full of bags and boxes. The crib would be delivered to the small town in a couple of weeks.

The ladies dropped Peyton off at her house, and the rest went to the hotel rooms they had reserved. Peyton felt so good to be back home with Dave again. It seemed like a long time since she they'd been together. She was pleased to see a positive change in him from when he had his accident, and they discussed it and his health issues as they talked into the night. He was surprising adept at using his crutches around the house, and he said he didn't use the wheelchair unless it was really needed. He assured Peyton that he was following his doctor's orders, keeping up with regular physiotherapy, and watching his diet because of the diabetes. He was eager to get well and get on with life.

Peyton had brought her laptop with updated pictures of the Lodge, and they studied them happily together. Dave was pleased with the progress that had been made and complemented for her good work. He asked about the workers she had hired and was pleased when she assured him that they were a good crew. She told him about foreman Tom too…how much it meant for him to leave his own business to help her with the project. Dave was impressed with it all. Not only did he enjoy hearing about the work on the Lodge, but about the people who had come into his daughter's life. Peyton found herself telling him about Tom and his company, his brother Allen "the prodigal son" who had made Tom an uncle by having a sweet baby girl, and Helen their mother, who Peyton regarded as a lovely lady.

Dave mused when they finally decided to call it a night. "You know, my dear, for a while after the accident I felt that it was all my fault, making me feal like a failure. But what has happened to me these past couple of months has been a blessing. I realized my accident could have been much worse, sailing into that ditch and into the tree. I could have been driving faster, smashed into the tree harder, or the truck could have flipped over. I feel blessed to be saved from what could have been my death. There's something else that changed my life. Having these weeks of forced rest gave me a chance to realize that I never truly grieved for your mom. When she passed, I couldn't handle it, and I pushed it out of my mind in various ways. I know you suffered from it. I tried to forget our loss with booze almost every night at the bar, not eating properly, sometimes not getting out of bed for days, other times working too hard so I wouldn't have to face it. I'm so sorry all that spilled over to you, sweetheart. Things did get better to a point, and we continued with our business, but having this extra time of mental reflection and physical healing has really been good for me. I feel that God has His hand on us with this new flip. As far as you're concerned, not only are you realizing how strong and competent you are on your own, but you have also met a fine man that you obviously have feelings for. Tom is just the type of person I would want for your partner in life. I do believe he's the one God wants for you."

Payton fought tears as her dad enveloped her in a bear hug, something she hadn't had from him in years. "I love you, and I'm so glad you're here. I've arranged for your friends to come here for brunch tomorrow, so we should get some sleep. Good night, my girl. Rest and be blessed."

For the first time in ages, Payton had a wonderful sleep in her own bed and woke to the smell of fried bacon. She was surprised at the time and hurriedly dressed, then packed another suitcase with a few more clothes to take back to the site. Looking through her closet, she decided to take a fancy dress and high heels as well. She hadn't worn a dress for a long time, but maybe an occasion would arise. A fleeting thought…wondering how Tom would react to see her in something more formal than t-shirts and jeans. Silly girl thoughts, but she folded the dress carefully and laid it on top anyway.

She heard voices from the kitchen and hustled downstairs. Dave was at the stove. A tall, slender woman of middle age was setting places at the dining room table. "Good morning, Dad. And who is this?"

"Ellie Mitchell." The woman turned with a smile and extended her hand. "Peyton, lovely to meet you. Your dad has told me so much about you." Peyton smiled and returned the greeting. "You're the nurse from the hospital! I recognize your voice. You're the one I spoke with the night Dad had the accident." She blushed. "I'm afraid I was pretty short with you."

"You were scared and I don't blame you. It must have been terrible for you at the time."

"It was. But you understood my feelings and reassured me. Thank you. I'm very grateful."

"Glad to be of help. That's my job." Ellie continued to set the table and Peyton sidled up to the stove. "Dad," she whispered. Is there something you haven't told me about?"

Dave reached for his crutches, then turned to her. "Ellie is the nurse that was on duty the night I was brought in by ambulance. She looked after me that night and arranged for me to talk with you the next morning." He smiled at Ellie. "She has been very helpful, both at the hospital and when I was released and brought home. She set up dates for physiotherapy for me do from home and it's helping a lot. She also arranged to have hot meals delivered to me by the church ladies. We've become good friends and I've discovered she's an amazing cook! I asked her to come over today to help me make brunch for you and your friends."

Just then the doorbell rang and Peyton went to answer it. The other three ladies entered with hugs for Peyton and chatter about their nice overnight hotel stay. Baby Jasmine in her car seat was immediately the centre of attention, charming everyone with her curls and toothless grin. Peyton introduced her father to everyone, and Ellie quickly added that she was a friend. When she turned away to finish setting the table, eyebrows were raised and Julie mouthed, "Who is she?" Peyton whispered, "I just met her myself."

The brunch was delicious and the conversation around the table interesting as the ladies asked about Dave's accident and current health, including Ellie's part in it. Dave & Ellie sat side by side and seemed relaxed and comfortable with the group. Dave was a happy host and proud Papa, entertaining them with talk about Peyton as a child, and her ambitious climb to a journeyman carpenter. Helen had a few stories about Tom that she shared, and Peyton enjoyed hearing them, though it was obvious to everyone that she was a matchmaker, focused on Peyton for her Tom. Although Peyton protested, she finally gave up and let them have their fun.

When Dave excused himself for a moment, Peyton followed suit and cornered him in the hallway. "Dad! Are you and Ellie in a relationship? Why didn't you tell me last night?"

Dave sighed. "I'm sorry. We talked about so much last night, and it was late, so I thought it best to wait. I didn't realize that Ellie was coming until this morning. She was on night shift last night and said she wasn't sure she would make it today. I'm very glad she did. I've wanted you to meet her for a long time."

"You are in a relationship?"

"Right now, we're just good friends, honey. But it's going to be more." He seemed slightly embarrassed but squared his shoulders. "You know how much I loved your mother. Still do, and I'll always treasure those memories. But I feel 100% better than I did a year ago, even with a broken leg. I think your mom would want me to move on. Ellie is a lovely person, don't you think?"

"Yes, she seems to be. I just wished you'd told me before today." She looked into his eyes. It was not the time to say any more about it, so Peyton let it go. "Of course, Dad, it's your life. Just be sure. I would hate to see you get hurt."

After a scrumptious breakfast the group took turns for hitting the bathroom before the trip home. On the way out, Peyton made a point of going to Ellie and giving her a smile and a hug, with thanks for the lovely meal. Once they were on the road back, she couldn't stop thinking about the situation. Helen had chosen the back seat again and promptly dozed off, as did Charlene and Jasmine. Julie looked over at Peyton and squeezed her hand. "You're a quiet one. Tired?"

"No, I'm just thinking about my dad. He's fallen in love with Ellie."

"Yeah, I kind of noticed." Julie smiled. "How do you feel about it?"

"She seems like a nice person, and she obviously thinks a lot of Dad. I guess I'm happy if he's happy. My mom's been gone for a long time now." She felt a lump in her throat and blinked back the tears. "Seeing Dad with another woman though, brought back memories. Mom's fight with cancer was terrible and it took a toll on Dad…on both of us. This morning was somewhat of a shock for me. But Dad hasn't been this happy for years. He deserves a partner to grow old with." If this was her dad's decision, she wouldn't stand in his way. It will make a huge difference for me, though."

THIRTEEN

Tom had finished clearing out his basement suite and it was now available for Allen and family to move in. Helen and Charlene had cleaned it from top to bottom and were now stocking the kitchen cupboards with dishes and food. Throughout the morning, family and friends from their church had been dropping by to help and take turns minding the baby. Although Charlene had been shy at first, she had opened like a flower when the ladies went to the city, and now seemed comfortable with everyone. Charlene's parents had let the couple store their belongings with them until they were settled somewhere, and now the truck had arrived from the east. Peyton volunteered to help by bringing lunch for the group, and there was some for everyone. After cleanup was over and the group was disbanding, Allen raised his hands and got their attention.

"Before you go, we just want to say a word to you all." He pulled Charlene close and she smiled up at him and the others around them. "You've given us such a warm welcome back to this community that we can't begin to express our thanks to you all." Allen's voice cracked and his eyes brimmed. "We're so grateful that you opened your hearts to make it possible for us to be in this beautiful home." He swiped his eyes and swallowed hard. "Growing up in this town, I didn't appreciate the love of my own family and friends. As you probably know, I made a mess of my life in the past, causing my mother and brother many sorrows, and I can't take that back. I wish I could. I tried to change many times and failed because I couldn't do it on my own. But my life changed when I met Charlene. She's a woman of faith, and with her support, I've become a better man. This past year I gave my heart to the Lord, and now He's giving me the strength that I need. He has guided us back home where He wants us to be. Thank you from the bottom of our hearts for your love and acceptance. And you, Tom, for allowing us to live in this lovely apartment. Thank you, Peyton for taking a chance on me and giving me a job. Thank you, all of you who have given us so much today. These gifts are a blessing. We look forward to being in this community."

There was hardly a dry eye as people hugged the young couple and wish them well. Tom gravitated to Peyton, who was also feeling emotional. "I'm so glad you made the decision you did, Tom. Your family and friends have been wonderful to Allen and Charlene, and I'm sure they're going to be very happy now that they have some roots. I'm a bit envious. I've never experienced such love and support. It's wonderful to see."

"I thought you and your parents attended a church where you grew up." Tom reached out and brushed a stray lock of hair from her face. "Don't you have friends there still?"

"We did attend a church regularly when I was young, but when I graduated from high school, and Dad and I started construction together, we often worked on Sundays to complete the projects on time, and Mom didn't like going to church by herself. When she was diagnosed with cancer, she couldn't leave the house at all. The chemo was just too hard on her. We drifted away from the church friends we had, and eventually stopped going entirely. Programs and activities were not what we needed when the times were that tough."

Peyton turned to smiled up at Tom. "This day has been wonderful. A small community of people who give so much of themselves to others. It's good to be with you all and feel your kindness. I will miss it when I go."

"Whoa, not so fast, little lady!" Tom laid a hand on her shoulder and put on a cowboy drawl. You're not leaving us yet and we still have time to convince you to stay. My mom has made it her personal mission to convince you of that. In case you haven't noticed, she's a hard person to say no to."

Peyton blushed and turned toward the people around them. "Yes, I did kind of get that impression. Really, it is a lovely town and you are all lovely people," she said lightly. "But I have my dad and our business to think about. We have several projects coming up in the city that we need to finish by the end of summer. I had a call this morning from a realtor who wants to know when he can list the Lodge. Julie will be doing that when the time comes, but other realtors are already hot on the trail. We need to ramp things up in the next couple of weeks so she can start showing the property."

Murmurs from a few folks showed their disappointment that Peyton would be leaving, but others were excited that the Lodge would soon be finished. Tom sighed, then turned back to her. "What do you think of my house?"

Peyton brightened. "We've been so busy this morning. It's beautiful. I'd love a tour." Not wanting to use the connecting door now that the young couple had the suite, Tom ushered her outside and around the front. Julie and Ed were leaving and waved from their car, as did Helen who was close behind. She gave them a thumbs up and a big smile. No doubt happy to see Peyton and Tom together.

Tom wanted Peyton to come in by his front door to get the full appearance of the entry. "I built this house five years ago, on an acre of land. After you, Madam." The front door was beautiful, with old world style hardware and a stained-glass window. The best was yet to come. She gasped with pleasure at the huge character log that graced the main foyer. It was over twenty feet high with a root base at least eight feet in diameter. "This is the log that holds up the whole house," Tom said proudly. "Without it, the whole thing would collapse."

"It's wonderful, Tom! Fantastic! It must be hundreds of years old. How on earth did you get it in here?"

"On a flat-bed truck. We had to use a crane to raise it. It weighs several thousand pounds. It had to go up first and then the rest of the house was built around it."

They wandered around the foyer and Tom pointed out the other character logs in various rooms. "This house was built right on this property, but the ones in our log yard are built there and then dismantled for shipment to wherever the customer wishes." He explained that his crews prepare the logs and number them one by one as they build. "When the construction is complete, everything gets dismantled and shipped to wherever the customer's property is. Our crews follow and then rebuild it on their site. Of course, the customer must build his foundation before we do our part. And it's up to the customer to hire a contractor of their choice to finish the rest of the build - roof, doors and windows, electricity and plumbing."

Peyton was amazed at the size and beauty of Tom's home. She loved the modern open plan kitchen and living area and the cozy stone fireplace. Light spilled through dozens of windows that framed views of trees and mountains. The bedrooms were on the second floor, accessed by a delightful log spiral staircase. Tom didn't have much furniture up there except in the master bedroom, which had a beautiful log four-poster bed with matching dressers. That room had a large picture window with a breath-taking view. She couldn't imagine Tom living by himself in such a big, beautiful house, and for five years? Plenty of room for a family. No wonder Helen and the other ladies were matchmaking.

"Like it?" Tom finished up the tour by ushering her downstairs to the kitchen. They sat on log stools at a beautiful wooden counter, and Tom made each of them a Keurig coffee. It really mattered to him what Peyton thought. She seemed to appreciate the craftsmanship and beauty of his home that meant so much to him. She'd been delighted with each part. Quite a difference from Tracey's abrupt visit a couple of weeks earlier. She had flopped on the couch and shown no more than a passing interest in his work of art.

"I love it, Tom!" Peyton gazed out the large window facing the back garden and its orderly rows of veggies, flowers and lawn. "Your yard is beautiful too. How do you find the time to care for everything?"

"As far as the yard goes, I hire Jason to do the outside work for the summer. That's how I knew he would do well at your job site. He's actually very good at gardening, and I think he has the aptitude for it. I've spoken to him about maybe taking horticulture in college." He chuckled. "As far as the inside of my house? I like it clean, and there's only Carver and I, so it doesn't get too dirty." He grinned at her. "My mom loves this place, and me, so she brings me goodies and does housework while she's here. Now that we have that sweet baby downstairs, Mom will be around here all the time."

Peyton smiled at his teasing. "Maybe, but doesn't your mom have the store to run?"

"To be honest, Mom has just been waiting for grandchildren as an excuse to retire. She's getting on in years and the hard work of the store is catching up with her. She can afford to have employees now and gives them responsibility."

Peyton sipped her coffee and couldn't help wondering why Tom hadn't married. Just from working with him over these past few weeks, observing his work ethics and attitude towards employees, involvement in his church and community, and love and concern for family members, she had to admit that he was a prize for any woman, yet he didn't seem interested. Perhaps he had a broken heart from someone…maybe Tracey. Or as Julie seemed to think, he was waiting for the right woman to come along. His standards were high, she was sure.

Watching him make the coffee, her heart skipped a beat as she imagined what it would be like to marry a man as fine as Tom. They were few and far between. She gave herself a mental shake. Here she was contemplating Tom as husband material when she herself had no intention of getting married any time soon. She had to look after her dad and their business above everything else now. Who knew how long it would be before Dave could be able to go back to work? Like Tom's mom, he was getting near retirement age for most people, and this accident had set him back quite a bit. There were several projects they committed to before his accident and Peyton knew she had a tough summer ahead. She should be getting back to work instead of daydreaming about living in this beautiful home. But now she didn't want this time with Tom to end, and it appeared he didn't want it either.

"Would you like to come and see how a log home is built? We have a big one under construction there now. The day is almost over for my guys so this is a good time to come to the site."

"I would love it, Tom." They finished up their coffee and Tom excused himself to see to the dog. Then Peyton had second thoughts. The drive to the log yard in Tom's truck would be a bit uncomfortable. What was she doing here with a guy so attractive that she could hardly keep her eyes off him? How had she allowed herself to be drawn into this circle of family that she was getting to know and care about? Soon the Lodge would be finished and put up for sale, and she would leave for another project. She shouldn't have gotten so emotionally involved with this town and these people. It wasn't like her to get so attached, but she'd been drawn into the lives of these folks one by one. And it was obvious that her new friends were getting attached to her as well. She chuckled, remembering Helen's happy grin and thumbs-up salute as she drove by them earlier. She would love to have Helen in her life. She hadn't had many women in her life since her mom died and she missed that. Helen had a handsome son that she was trying to match up with Peyton and that made leaving all the harder. Peyton couldn't let that happen. She had to stop those feelings from getting any stronger.

Tom looked over at her and smiled. "You're quiet. It's been a long day, hasn't it? Why don't we leave the site tour for another day and just grab some supper in town? Then maybe see what's on at the theatre?"

That sounded like a date to Peyton and as much as she would like to do that with Tom, she knew she had to start pulling away before the ties got any stronger. "I'm pretty tired. I think I'll just head back to the Lodge. I've got a bunch of invoices to pay and we've got to catch up to schedule since we took the day off today."

"Yeah, I guess you're right." Tom seemed disappointed. "Do you want me to give you a lift?"

"No need. I'll just walk back to the Lodge. I need to stretch my legs." She assured him with a warm smile that the day had been wonderful. He came nearer to her and she suddenly felt tears coming. She blinked them away with a little laugh, passing it off as the emotion of earlier in the day. Tom suddenly reached out and took her hand. "Thank you for coming today, Peyton. The whole community thinks you're wonderful, including me. You've blended in so well that you've managed to capture all our hearts."

"Thanks, Tom. I feel the same way about all of you. But I do have to leave, soon." She squeezed his hand and then pulled hers free. She had to get out of here before she broke down. "Thanks for letting me tour your home. It's just fabulous. See you tomorrow."

Tom followed her to the door and watched her walk down the driveway, with Carver at her side. She leaned down and quickly hugged the beautiful dog, then a quick whistle brought the retriever running back to Tom. Peyton walked away and was soon out of sight. He felt suddenly bereft and realized with a pang that after all these years, something had happened. He had finally fallen in love. Why did it have to be someone who's home was 300 miles away, and a career and lifestyle so different from his?

FOURTEEN

The next day, with the renos inside the Lodge relatively complete, and professionals busy laying new floorings, Peyton turned her attention to the landscaping, a huge factor when people purchased a property. She asked Ed and Julie to help, since they loved gardening and had a lovely yard of their own. Peyton welcomed the extra help since she wasn't experienced herself. The grounds of the Lodge had been neglected for years and she needed all the help she could get.

Jason was home from school and doing a good job on the lawns. Peyton had met his parents at Allen's housewarming and they seemed happy to know their boy was doing well at the project site. Jason was a worry for them at times but it was obvious he enjoyed working at the Lodge. Giving him a chance to shine at what he liked to do could be just what the young man needed to boost his self-esteem. Peyton was happy to help him with that.

They decided to make a trip to the town's garden center. The store was huge and beautiful! Peyton didn't know where to start, but she was amazed at how much Jason and Julie knew about plants suited for the mountain climate. She purchased a colorful mixture of spring and summer annuals, as well as several hardy perennials, fertilizer, topsoil and mulch to add to the plants at the acreage. The back of Ed's truck was full to the top when they headed back.

Peyton was having a hard time keeping Tom from her mind. She hadn't seen him for a few days, and she missed him. Things were going well and the closer they got to finishing, the more she realized the project would soon be completed. She hadn't realized until now how much she depended on Tom and enjoyed his company. Almost every day when he passed the work site, he would either toot the truck horn or stop in for a quick coffee, some days even staying several hours to help when needed. She had to admit that she was beginning to care for him. Not only because of his help with the renovations but as a friend and confidant. She was paying him for the time that he and his employees spent on her project, and she was immensely grateful for that. If not for Tom's generosity in the absence of her father, they would have had to scrap the project until Dave was healthy again, and who knew when that would be? It would have been a financial disaster for their business. But now she was realizing that Tom was meant much more to her. He'd drawn her into his circle of family and friends, lightening the load she felt as a stranger in town. She dreaded the day approaching when the job would be finished and turned over to Julie for the real estate listing. Not only did she love the Lodge, she fell in love with the contractor who had helped so much to make it beautiful again.

Soon Julie and Jason were hard at work, digging and turning, enriching the soil and placing the plants as Julie directed. Peyton wasn't much help at first, but once things started to take shape, she grew more interested.

"This is going to be wonderful, guys!" She was rewarded with a grin from Jason, who was sweaty and dirty but obviously having a great time. "Are we going to have enough to fill the flower beds?"

"Don't you worry." Julie straightened up. "I'm sure there's plenty and if not, we can do another quick run into town. I'm sure glad you have today off from school, Jason. You're a big help. We've got it covered out here. How are things going inside?"

"Good! I brought stuff to make lunch for everyone today so I'll go in and get that started. Sandwiches and cold drinks for everyone." Just then her cell phone rang, with her dad on the line. She hadn't talked to him for a week and was pleased to hear from him.

"Hey, Dad. I've been thinking about you. How are you?"

"I'm doing well. Just came from the doctor's office and he says I'm healing pretty good. So well in fact that he says it's okay for me to come and see you."

"Really? That's great! I'd love that. How will you get here?"

"Ellie has some time off coming to her, so she's going to drive me. She has friends who live in another town not far from there so she'll drop me off and go to spend a few days with them."

Peyton let out a breath of thanks. It would be a bit awkward to have Ellie staying at the site and she was pleased that she would have Dave to herself.

"When are you coming, Dad?"

"If all goes well, we'll be there tomorrow afternoon."

"Wonderful! I'm excited for you to see the place, Dad. You'll be amazed at all the beautiful changes. Right now, we have a guy sanding the great room floor. We found beautiful wood underneath all that linoleum. Most of the upstairs rooms are done and the rest should be finished tomorrow. Just a few more things to finish on the main floor, mostly in the kitchen. In a week or so, we should be ready to list."

Dave was excited too. "You've been showing me things online but it's not the same as being there. I'm itching to see you and the Lodge in person."

"I've been missing you a lot, Dad. I can't wait for hugs. See you tomorrow then. Love you!"

Julie looked up from her work and smiled at Peyton. "Good news, eh? I'm happy for you."

"Yes, Dad's coming tomorrow afternoon. I'll start cleaning up in the Lodge the best I can once these guys are done. I'm hoping Dad will be able to sleep in the motorhome. He might have trouble with the stairs."

"We have a cot that we can bring over for you so he can sleep in the Lodge. The plumbing and heating are all done, aren't they? Or he and Ellie could stay at our house."

"I think we'll be okay. Sleeping in the Lodge by himself wouldn't be very nice. There's room in the motorhome and we can probably get him in and out. Thankfully, Ellie is dropping him off here and going to stay with a friend. I don't have to deal with that situation." She avoided Julie's eyes. "I know...I have to learn to accept his relationship with her. But it's difficult."

"I know," Julie soothed. "But you'll get there. Dave is obviously happy and you need to be happy for him, in the long run. I liked them both when we met at your house. Your dad seems to have a good head on his shoulders. And Ellie was very respectful of you and your feelings." She paused and suddenly brightened. "I just had an idea. Would you like us to make dinner for you all at our house while they're here? We can make it a party to celebrate the completion of the project. Invite Tom and Helen, and maybe Allen and Charlene as well!"

A farewell dinner. Peyton's eyes filled and she

chuckled when Julie reached over with a hug. "Would you? That would be awesome. I sure can't entertain in the motorhome. And once the Lodge is cleaned and ready, the place will be staged, so I wouldn't want to mess that up." She felt a lump in her throat to think they were that close to finishing the project and leaving town.

Julie pulled off her garden gloves. "I'll work on it once we get this done. How long is your dad staying?"

"Just a few days from the sound of it, but I'm not sure. We'll know more when he gets here." She reached out for a hug. "Thank you, Julie. You've been such a help to me and to everyone."

"You're welcome. I don't know why I'm planning a going-away party for you. I don't want you to be finished. It's way too soon! Wouldn't you love to stay here permanently? I'm sure there's work for carpenters around here."

Peyton grinned. "Sure! I could get a job at Tom's company. That's carpentry extraordinary! And I bet the pay is good."

"Now you're talking, girl! Seriously though, honey. You've said yourself that you love this area. You can come and live with Ed and I. We have a basement suite that you could live in until you find a job and a place of your own."

"How could I do that, Julie? Dad and I have a thriving business in the city. This hick-cup with his accident needs to be corrected and then continued. A lot of business is waiting to be done at home." Something that she would have to discuss with Dave when he came. The thought saddened her. She didn't want to go back to the city or to her life there. To lose her new friends and this beautiful place would be the hardest thing she could ever do. And leaving Tom would break her heart.

Peyton stayed up well into the evening, working in

the Lodge, sweeping and mopping the dust from the new floors and cleaning up debris left in other areas of the renovations. She wanted the place to look as nice as possible, even though there was still a bit of work to be done. She sat down and made a list that was surprisingly short. The loft rooms had already been painted, flooring put down, and doors and new windows installed. On the second floor, all the bedroom and bathroom walls had been painted and new flooring put down everywhere. New baseboards still had to be installed in each of them. Vanities and fixtures for each bathroom should be arriving within the week, as well as the sinks for kitchen and utility rooms, and the kitchen equipment. Tom had built the kitchen cupboards from reclaimed lumber and put them up. The doors for them would be arriving in the delivery.

In another week or two the Lodge would be ready for staging. Soon Julie would be arranging for the local furniture store to lend some furniture and she would provide smaller items from her own home to make the place look nice. The antique tables and chairs in the great room would help with the showing. Thankfully, they had been covered to protect them over the years, so just a bit of dusting would be all that was needed. Because the Lodge was so huge, they would not be able to stage very much in other rooms, except maybe a couple of the bedrooms.

When she had done as much as she could, and was ready to lock up, Peyton was surprised to hear a knock at the door and Tom's voice. "Saw the lights on when I was going by, and thought I would pop in. What are you doing here at this hour?"

"I could ask you the same question," she chuckled. "Coming home from a date?"

Tom locked eyes with her and flipped a finger under her chin. "I don't date." He smiled. "Not unless it's with you."

"Since when did we have a date?" Peyton teased and turned away so he wouldn't see her blush.

"Well, I took you to out to dinner, once. At my mom's, but that's still taking you out."

"Yes, you did. And I enjoyed it very much. There's coffee in the thermos. Want some?"

"No thanks. I've been eating junk food and pop at the Youth Group movie night. Anymore and I'll burst."

Peyton sighed. "Remember the night you came to my door after dark bearing gifts of chili and groceries? How long has it been…maybe nine or ten weeks?"

"Yeah, about that. But it seems like yesterday. I heard an ugly rumor that soon you're going to be leaving. Tell me it's not true."

"I'm afraid it is." She couldn't meet his eyes and busied herself wiping a counter that she'd already done several times. "My dad is coming tomorrow. He wants to inspect the place and we'll spend some time talking about the next steps. There's really not much left to be done before we get Aunt Julie puts it up for sale."

Tom grabbed a folding chair and straddled it. "Julie called me and told me about the dinner she's planning. She called it a celebration but I don't think it is. I won't be celebrating."

"I know. Me too. I love this place. When I think back over the last couple of months, I realize how blessed I've been." She turned to face him and her eyes were brimming. "Dad's accident nearly bowled me over when I heard about it, and if it hadn't been for Julie recommending you help me with everything, I don't know what I would have done. Packed up and gone back home, I guess, or listed the lodge for sale again the way it was. You came to my rescue. You were my rock when I needed one, and I can't tell you how much that means to me."

Tom gazed at her and took her hand. "It's meant a lot to me to get to know you, and work with you on this project. You've become my good friend and almost part of my family now." He cleared his throat. "Peyton, we could be more to each other if you'd let me. Won't you consider staying a bit longer?"

"I can't, Tom." Her voice was barely a whisper. "Believe me, I've been thinking about it for a while. How happy I've been to meet your family and be included in everything. I've never had a family like yours and it's been wonderful. And I treasure the closeness I've felt when we've been together. The thought of going back to the city and living at home with my dad depresses me. The city is where our work is, and my dad is depending on me to keep our business going until he gets well." Her cheeks were wet with tears. "I've never lived on my own and I will have to do that if he marries Ellie. But I have to go back."

Tom stood up and took her in his arms. "I care for you, Peyton. I've been attracted to you ever since we first met, and my feelings have grown stronger each day. I've never known a woman like you, and I realize now that you're the one I've been waiting for my whole life. We would be happy together, I know it."

Peyton raised her eyes to his, and he leaned down to kiss her lips. At the last moment she pulled away as she knew she had to. "You are a wonderful man, Tom, and any woman would be proud to have you as a husband. I have feelings for you too, Tom, but I have to think about my dad now. He's the only family I have, and I can't let him down. Please understand. You can't leave your family and business here, and I can't leave my father and our business there. Long distance relationships are difficult and that's what it would have to be. And I don't think it would work."

Tom's eyes searched her face and then reluctantly released her. "We could if we wanted it badly enough. I won't forget this moment and I hope you won't either. Good night, Peyton."

FIFTEEN

Peyton hardly slept that night, and when she dozed, she dreamed of Tom. After tossing and turning in the wee hours, she got up and dressed. She had given the crew the day off and wanted everything to be as nice as possible when her father arrived. Although he had given a lot of input to the renovations via phone calls and online photos, Peyton felt that this was going to be an important step in their partnership. His approval meant more to her than any positive feedback from new friends and hired employees. If what she had accomplished wasn't as good as what Dave would do, she would be failing him.

Since Tom had been such a big part of the renovations, Peyton asked him to come over in the afternoon to be there when Dave and Ellie arrived. Knowing she would be on edge, he came earlier, with a basket of sandwiches and soft drinks. "Thought you'd be too busy this morning to eat properly so I brought a picnic lunch to make sure you would."

"Thank you, Tom. You're right…I didn't eat breakfast and I'm famished." She avoided his eyes and there was an awkwardness between them now that she regretted. But it couldn't be helped.

Tom noticed she had changed from her normal jeans and T-shirt to a pretty-flowered dress and let her auburn hair curl down around her shoulders instead of being in a ponytail. "You look lovely today."

She smiled her thanks. "I feel like a kid on Parent-Teacher night. I've never been in this position before, wanting my dad's approval of such a big project. I'm very nervous."

"Listen, you don't have anything to worry about. You've done a stellar job with this place, and it's gorgeous. You've improved it 200% from what it was when you bought it. I especially like the master suite and office up in the loft that you added. The entry way is beautiful, now that everything is clean and polished, and replacing that fireplace in the great room with a proper wood burner was a great idea."

"Yes, it does make a big difference, doesn't it?" Peyton smiled as she looked around. "I was up until two this morning. Would you like to see upstairs before they come?"

"If you eat a sandwich or two first. I'll show you how it's done." Peyton couldn't help but laugh as Tom grabbed a cheese sandwich and took a huge bite. "Now you." He tossed a plastic lunch bag at her.

They stayed together for the next hour, chatting about what was left to do and the nice job Julie and Jason were doing in the yard. Peyton could feel the tension easing away in Tom's presence. He was good at doing that to her, had been ever since they first met. They made a good team, no doubt about it. She pushed away the sad thoughts of not having that anymore.

When they were upstairs admiring things, they heard a car in the driveway. "Here they are!" Peyton took a deep breath and smoothed her hair as they descended the front stairs. Ellie was getting out of the driver's seat and flashed a smile at them as she opened the trunk to get

Dave's crutches. Peyton and Tom helped Dave struggle to his feet and get a hug from his daughter. Once equipped and on his feet, he gazed around at the mowed lawns and flower beds, and the towering pine trees.

"Wow! This looks a whole lot better than when we first saw this place."

"Doesn't it? And we're still not quite finished. There's a bit more to be done in the rest of the yard."

Ellie was all smiles, hugging Peyton and shaking hands with Tom. "This is a beautiful spot. I can see now why you bought it."

"Would you like to sit down in the great room first? You must be tired from your drive."

"Not at all!" Dave was already looking around and admiring the beautiful woodwork in the entry way. "Cleaned up all of this, eh? Looks beautiful. And I see that someone made the check-in counter as lovely as the rest. Ready for customers!"

"Have a look at the back yard first, Dad. Lots of woodland, nice and shady. Our crew did a great job restoring the deck yesterday. Just in time for your visit." Julie had provided a few lounge chairs as part of her staging, and Dave sat down with Ellie helping him lift his leg. "Interesting!" Dave commented. "There's a lot of space back there. Enough that the owner could build several cabins for those that want more privacy."

Dave was surprisingly agile with his crutches, as they admired the beautiful setting behind the Lodge and then went back in through the new sliding doors. Tom had cleaned up the remnants of their lunch so the kitchen would be tidy and was rewarded by a grateful smile from Peyton. Dave was enthralled when they entered the main area. "Wonderful! I see you've polished up the woodwork. Gorgeous! When we bought the Lodge, we were pleased that it hadn't been painted over. I love the open plan, so popular today." He balanced on one crutch and reached an arm out to squeeze Peyton to him. "I'm really impressed, honey."

Tom was with Ellie in the background and Peyton sought him out with her eyes and beckoned him. "I have to give a lot of credit to Tom, Dad. He's been so generous with his help and advice at times. And taking his own time and crews to work with me. We couldn't have done this flip without his support."

"Of course! Tom, I'm immensely grateful. I'm so sorry that I couldn't have been here to work with you. My daughter has been singing your praises from the beginning. Sounds like you've gone above and beyond your duty. Thank you so much!"

"It's been my pleasure, Sir." He reached out to shake hands. "Peyton is a remarkable woman and very good at what she does. I'm happy to work with her."

Although it took some effort, Dave insisted on climbing the stairs to see the second and third floors, glowing praise for what he saw. "Not only is my daughter a proficient carpenter but she has a flair for decorating. These bathrooms are top notch. And I love how the loft turned out. I was surprised when Peyton told me that she wanted to clear it out and make a couple of rooms. I thought it was only good as a storage place. It looks great!"

Tom had borrowed a few folding chairs from the church, set up around the great room fireplace when they came back downstairs. He and Peyton went to the motorhome and brought back coffee and fixings, as well as a platter of pastries and fruit for everyone. Ellie stayed for a bit, then excused herself to continue the drive to her friend's home a few miles away. She pecked Dave on the cheek and stroked his arm on the way out. Peyton couldn't help noticing the eye contacts they made. There was definitely a relationship there.

Tom went with Ellie to get Dave's things from her car. Peyton asked her dad if he would be able to get in and out of the motorhome, or if he would prefer to stay with Julie and Ed. He said he was fine in the motorhome, which was his second home. He was quite willing to walk around everywhere. "It's amazing what they have now in the medical field. The boot I'm wearing is fitted with little plastic airbags, custom made for my foot so I can put some weight on it when necessary. I should be fine."

When Tom got back, the talk continued about the Lodge and what the next steps would be once everything was completed. Other customers' flips were waiting their turn in the city for Dave and Peyton. Instead of being interested, Peyton felt a cloud descending. She wasn't ready to leave this one behind. They had put a lot of time and energy into flipping other homes. But this one was different. She was leaving not only the beautiful Lodge they had refurbished, but part of herself that had become intertwined with the community. People she had grown fond of. She knew that at the top of that list was Tom.

Dave asked about Tom's business and he was happy to talk about it. Dave was keenly interested in log homes and Tom offered to take him to the site. "I've been planning to take Peyton there and we haven't gotten around to it yet. If you're up to it, Sir, we could go tomorrow afternoon, and then top it off with a barbecue at my place. My own home is a log house that I built five years ago. I'd love for you see a finished product."

"That sounds great, Tom. But none of this 'sir' stuff. Please call me Dave."

Tom got to his feet and stretched out a hand to the

older man. "All right, Sir. Dave it is. I should be getting back to work myself, so I'll say good-bye for now and I'll see you tomorrow afternoon, say around two?" He looked to Peyton who confirmed with a nod and smile. "Is there anything else I can do for you?"

"Nope! I'm rather pooped from the long drive and I think I'd like a nap, if you don't mind, Kitten?"

"Of course not, Dad." She was grateful when Tom stayed to help get Dave into the motorhome, although it was surprisingly easy for him to maneuver the steps himself. Once he was aboard, Peyton walked with Tom to his vehicle.

"Do you have food in the motorhome for your supper? You can come to my place if you like."

"That's OK, Tom. I have lots of groceries. Thanks for coming today. I really appreciate you being here. You and my dad seem to get along well."

"I enjoyed it too. He is so proud of you. It was wonderful to see his delight with what you've accomplished."

"You mean what *we* have accomplished. I could not have done this without you, Tom. Believe me and take some credit."

Tom took her hand and looked into her eyes with a smile. "Yeah, we make a good team." He lifted her hand and brushed it with his lips, then slowly leaned forward. Peyton felt herself responding as Tom pulled her gently into his arms. For a moment she was lost in what was happening, then Tom gently pulled away. "I must go, before I do something I shouldn't." He brushed a lock of hair away from her face. "I'll see you tomorrow."

Peyton was shaken at what just happened Tears welled up in her eyes in a mix of wonder and sorrow. She had longed for this moment, ever since she realized her love for Tom. She should never have gotten into this situation. Why did she let her relationship with him go this far? The warmth of their friendship was more than that. Something she had always dreamed of, but now their feelings for one another had become the worst thing that could have happened.

We're from two different worlds and there is no way out of the situation but for me to distance myself. I needed to go back home to the city and put this all behind me. Get an apartment of my own. Maybe go back to school for an additional trade. Start on the next job with her dad as soon as he is well enough. Maybe even meet someone else. Although a little voice inside her insisted that she would never find another man as wonderful as Tom.

SIXTEEN

The log yard at Tom's business was bustling when they arrived the next afternoon. The office building was a beautiful structure adorned with a unique log arch above the main entrance, an advertisement itself of the quality products the company produced. There were several steps to the veranda but Dave managed them with no help, and they were rewarded with an interesting view over the yard. Huge Red Cedar logs were stacked everywhere with workmen in various stages of skinning, peeling, sanding and varnishing. Other trees with roots still attached were being moved around by heavy equipment with big tongs.

"Where do you get the logs from?" Peyton wanted to know.

"We buy them from other logging companies. We choose damaged ones if possible and the focus is on ones with character and natural beauty. We have machines that peel the logs, but for the character ones, we hand-peel." He pointed over toward a structure. "See that one we're building over there? That ridgepole weighs 5,000 pounds. Some of the really big ones are a lot more than that."

"You build the framework here and then take it apart again to take it to the customer?"

"That's correct, Dave. The customer decides what he

wants, with the help of our architect, then hires his own contractor to do the foundation on his site. We build the log portion here to the customer's specifications, numbering each piece as we go along. Then we take it apart, and transport the whole works to his property, wherever that might be, even if it's overseas. The crew goes with it and when we get there, we put it back together. We do all the log work and the customer's contractor finishes the roof, windows, plumbing and all that stuff."

"Wow, that's amazing. Quite the job. What keeps the logs together?"

Tom smiled. "Did you ever have a Lincoln Log set when you were a boy? It's something like that. We use dowels, and the logs are carefully cut out in V shapes to stack on one another. We insulate the grooves to keep in the heat and we put a sealer on the ends. And we look for unusual markings or shapes on the beams to make the house interesting. No two homes are ever the same."

"What kind of training do your employees have, to do this kind of work?" Ellie asked.

"All of them have done apprenticeships and are journeymen in Carpentry, Heavy Timber Framing and Log Construction."

After introducing them to other staff members in the office, Tom offered Dave a golf-cart ride around the yard. Peyton and Ellie opted to remain in the office and chat with the receptionist, Carrie, who was more than willing to gossip about her boss. "We all love Tom,'" she gushed. "Besides being handsome, he's the fairest, honorable, and caring employer I've ever had, and I'm sure the rest of the staff would say the same. I've never heard him say a harsh word to anyone. If there's a problem, he remains calm and works things out with the person." She cocked her head and looked Peyton up and down. "It just dawned on me that you're the reason he's been cutting back his hours here for another project. We've been speculating what the attraction is that would take him away from here that much. You're it!" She gave Peyton a wide smile. "About time that man got himself a sweetheart. He deserves it."

Peyton blushed and opened her mouth to disagree, but just then the door chimed and in walked Tom and Dave. "Saved by the bell," Peyton muttered, and Carrie gave her a big wink.

On the way back to Tom's house, Peyton reflected on the afternoon. She had been quite subdued, avoiding Tom's eyes, leaving him and Dave to chat. She couldn't stop thinking about the day before. Her heart was telling her that she had been attracted to Tom ever since they first met in the driveway of the Lodge. It was true that they had only known each other for a few weeks, but they had spent many hours working together at the Lodge, sharing intimate details of their families, and growing a friendship that she treasured. Carrie's comments came back to her. Everyone she knew loved Tom and respected him. Was Peyton a sweetheart to Tom?

Dave was so impressed with Tom's business that it made her wonder. "Thanks for the tour, Tom. It's been very interesting. Your employees seem very fond of you, especially Carrie."

"Is that so!" Tom chuckled. "I don't know about that. She's married. I just treat everyone like I would be like to be treated. They're a good bunch and we get along very well."

"Well, it's a fine business you have here, son." Dave gave Tom a pat on the back. I can't wait to see what you've done with your own home."

SEVENTEEN

Tracey appreciated her free week at the motel and she was thankful. But now the time was up and she worried about what to do next. It would be great if Tom just continued paying for her room, or even better, let her stay at his house for a while, but she didn't think that would happen. He hadn't been in touch with her since he dropped her off, and all week she'd been avoiding contact with the owner Andre, as much as she could. She felt like a nobody. She was used to getting her own way with everyone - her parents, her husband and Maria the housekeeper, but now no one wanted anything to do with her. She had tried to contact her parents but the housekeeper coldly told her that they were in France, wouldn't be back for six months, and had been ordered not to take calls from anyone. She was angry with them but knew her parents were finally doing what they had threated to do – make her live life on her own.

Tracey finally got up enough nerve to go to the office to talk to Andre. "Good morning!"

He looked up from behind the counter and smiled at her. "Checking out, are you?"

"Um…not exactly. I need another week here. I'm in a bit of a jam. My bank has messed up my account…a hacker, probably… and it's frozen right now. I'm waiting for a money transfer from my parents, but they're overseas and I can't get ahold of them."

Andre's smile faded and he frowned at her. "That's not what Tom told me when he paid for your room last week. He said you were desperate and had no money at all."

Tracey flushed and turned away from him. "He doesn't know everything. But it's true, I'm in a pickle. Unless Tom pays you for another week, I'm stranded. Are you going to kick me out?"

"Maybe, maybe not. You're in luck. I may have something to help you out. One of our chambermaids called in this morning. She's pregnant and not feeling well. Probably won't be coming back to work for at least a couple of weeks. I could use someone to take her place."

"A chambermaid? What is that?" Tracy was suspicious.

"Someone who cleans everything in the rooms for the customers. Changes the beds, cleans and sanitizes everything - bathrooms, toilets and bathtubs - vacuums the carpets, and takes the garbage out. Helping anywhere else needed...the works."

"How much are you paying?"

"Nothing, but you'll get your room for free until Carla comes back. Not sure when she'll be back. You would take her shift. 7am to 3pm."

Tracey gulped. She was used to getting up at ten or eleven in the morning, doing whatever she liked during the day, and then staying up late into the night. Ever since she was a little girl, Maria had looked after the child, and their home, keeping everything clean and tidy, making the beds for everyone, every morning. Tracy wasn't sure she could do any of the things Andre stated. But what else could she do? She would give it a try. It would probably be only for a few weeks, until the other woman came back to work, and then she would find something better. And at least she would have a roof over her head and make some money. She hated sleeping in her car or worse - having to sell it. "Okay, when do I start?"

"Right now. You'll need to change into different clothes. There are uniforms in the laundry room so go get one and change, then come back to me and I'll get another staff member to show you the ropes."

Andre smiled to himself as he watched her walk back to her room in her spike heels. Having Tracey as an employee might be very interesting.

EIGHTEEN

A fter a barbecue at Tom's, Dave and Peyton went back to the motorhome and spent a restful evening. It felt so good to be together again, and they chatted about lots of things...the project of course, and how nice the drive out was. Being this close to the Rockies was what they both loved, recalling the good times they'd had there in the past. Dave told her that Ellie had never been to the National Park and had expressed an interest in going there, but she only had two or three days off so they would have to go another time. Peyton mentioned a Dark Sky Festival that was coming up in the summer and Dave was interested. Perhaps they would come back to visit then if they weren't busy doing a flip.

"I had a visit from the RCMP last week about my accident."

"Really? How come?"

"Apparently some people saw my accident. I was so busy trying to keep the truck on the road, I never noticed the car or saw the other driver. Because I hit the tree and was knocked unconscious, I didn't know if anyone stopped to help, but apparently a young couple stopped and called 911, then stayed with me until the ambulance arrived. I guess the police are looking into it now."

"That's good. I suppose the truck was a total wreck?"

"Oh, yeah! When I was able to get out of hospital, Ellie took me to the scrap yard and I saw it. It looked terrible… almost made me sick remembering the crash. Thankfully, someone took our stuff out of the truck before it was taken away. I was worried that people would steal it out there on the highway. But everything was saved and it's all in our garage at home now. The truck's insured but it's pretty old so I won't get much for it."

"Maybe the couple that stopped would remember what the vehicle looked like. You don't remember anything about it? Was it a car or a truck? What color was it? Was someone in the passenger seat?"

"It was a car for sure." Dave frowned and stroked his beard. "The color? It was black, I think. I didn't see anyone else, only someone coming up fast in my rearview mirror. I knew it was going too fast and too close to me. And then the driver pulled out to pass but a deer ran across from the median and he swerved back over to me. Everything happened so fast. I tried to get out of the way but he yelled and kept coming over to me. I heard scraping and he pushed me hard. That's when my wheels caught the gravel and sucked me into the ditch. For a moment I thought I was going to roll over because the ditch was really deep. I managed to keep up but headed straight for a tree. Couldn't do anything but hang on."

Peyton shuddered and reached over to grasp Dave's hand. She could see he was getting upset. "That's awful, Dad. Thank the Lord for His protection. It could have been much worse if the truck had rolled. You did your best and saved your life."

"That's true. But I sure would like to have a word or two with that driver. It was so dark…I don't even know if it was a man or woman driving. Whoever it was, they made a big mistake travelling so fast at night."

"I'm so sorry, Dad. Perhaps the RCMP will have more information for you when you get home."

"Actually, I'm not worrying about that now. What's done is done. I'm thinking more about the finances of the project because I'll have to chat with the bank about it soon. You and your workers are doing a wonderful job with the Lodge, although once everything completed, and we put it up for sale, I'm sure they'll give us some more time."

The next evening was the promised dinner at Julie and Ed's home. Julie meant for it to be special and suggested that everyone dress their best. Peyton was impressed with Tom's navy sport jacket, shirt and tie, and noticed that his black curls were trimmed. She was glad she had brought her fancy dress from home. She looked stunning in the emerald gown with her long auburn curls framing her face. She was pleasantly surprised that Julie had invited Tom and Helen, Allen and Charlene, Jason and his parents and Tom's crew members who had worked on the renovation.

Julie and Ed's home was huge and a lovely setting for the party. The meal was a delicious buffet and the company wonderful, an evening with lots of chatter, laughter and stories. The locals knew each other well and enjoyed meeting for the evening, and it was lovely how they drew Peyton and her family into the circle. Tom looked relaxed, chatting and joking with his friends, and including his Helen in the conversations. It was obvious that his mother loved him very much and vice versa. What was the old saying? If you want a good husband, watch how he treats his mother. Peyton couldn't help but sneaking looks at Tom, and she caught his eyes on her as well many times during the evening.

Eventually Peyton noticed that her dad was looking tired. She drew Julie aside and they agreed that they should wind the evening down. Allen noticed too, and Charlene agreed that it was time to take Jasmine home. Julie stood up and tapped her glass to make an announcement.

"Folks, I think our sweet baby here needs to go home, and we need our beauty sleep too. I'm so glad you all came. It's been a lovely evening. Before you go, I just want to say a few words. As you know, I wanted to get together tonight to honor my niece who has been with us these three last months. She and her dad came to our community to take on the task of beautifying that rundown eye-sore Lodge in our town. Before they even got here, due to an unfortunate accident of no fault of his own, Dave was seriously injured, and was taken back home to rehabilitate. We're so glad to have you here tonight, Dave, to see you on the road to recovery. However, Peyton was faced with the challenge of managing this large project herself. If that had happened to me, I would have turned around and high-tailed it back to the city for good. But Dave and Peyton decided they would not do that. Peyton hired a local crew and got to work, and I'm so proud of what you've all accomplished. With prayers, coaching by phone and the internet, volunteer labor and other support from the community, we've all done a wonderful job! As you know, it is a flip and the property is going on the market in three weeks. It is so beautiful, I'm sure it will go fast. And soon, unfortunately, Peyton and Dave will be leaving us to go on to do projects in other places. It's been wonderful for me to have my niece so close for all this time and when you leave, we will miss you both terribly!"

Dave reached out a hand to his daughter. "I'm so proud of my girl. It was an enormous job to take on but I knew she was capable of doing it."

"We've had a lot of help, Dad. Many of you folks have contributed your time and expertise to the job. I would especially like to thank my very capable foreman Tom, who came to my rescue at the very beginning and provided me with knowledge, time and labor from his own business. We could not have made all this happen without him. Thank you, Tom, and all of you. We will never forget your kindness."

Julie raised her wine glass in salute and everyone followed, clinking with one another. It had been a lovely time with everyone and she waved away the guests who offered to help with clean-up. "Ed and I will take care of that, don't you worry. We're just so happy you came."

As the folks began to get ready to leave, Peyton dared not meet Tom's eyes, for she knew she would break down. She blinked back tears as folks came to hug her, and she eventually managed to say goodbye to Julie in the kitchen. Helen was trying to give Tom and Peyton the opportunity to drive home together on their own, but Dave and Peyton accepted Ed's offer since he was tired and wanted to get back quickly. When Peyton was ready to leave, she looked for Tom but he had already left.

The next morning Ellie arrived back at the Lodge and she and Dave set off for the city. Peyton was sad to see them go but knew there were things that still needed to be done, so it was just as well. Julie was bringing a group of realtors in the afternoon to view the Lodge and she wanted everything to be perfect.

Allen was working with Peyton today, helping her frame a pantry off the kitchen, cutting and hammering two-by-fours, slitting gyprock, and measuring wood for shelves. He had turned out to be a hard worker and Peyton was pleased. Wherever he was assigned to work in the project, he got right to it. When he was given his first paycheck, his eyes had widened at the amount Peyton gave him. He had earned it.

"How are you and Charlene doing, Allen? Enjoying your new home?"

"Oh yes, we love it. It's wonderful to have such a lovely place after the ones we've lived in before. We've moved around a bit since we first met, and the only rentals we could afford were in rough shape, in areas that were not safe. I'm so thankful for what Tom is giving us. We're getting his suite rent-free right now but as soon as we can, we're going to start paying for it. We want to stay as long as we can."

"Tom told me that this town is where you and Tom grew up. Were you happy here?"

"Oh yes. I have good memories of my childhood up until I was about eight. My dad worked for a company that sent him all over the place, even up to the up to the Arctic Circle, and we wouldn't see him for months at a time. He would keep in touch, though. He would send us frequent postcards and sometimes have flowers delivered to Mom, and always sent gifts for our birthdays. We loved it when he came home for a few weeks but then he'd and take off to somewhere else. Then one day he left for good. Tom and I were at school when he picked up his things for the last time. He didn't even wait to say goodbye to us kids. Mom wouldn't tell us why, and she hasn't told us to this day. Tom was angry for a long time, but I was too young to understand. Occasionally I get a memory and think about him. The whole thing broke Mom's heart though, and I guess Tom's too."

"That's sad! Does he live in this town? Do you see each other?"

"I have no idea. It's been many years since he left. We've never seen or heard from him again. He could have another family somewhere else. Maybe that's why he travelled so much. But he could be dead, who knows?"

"I hope I'm not being too nosy. But are you and Tom close?"

"When I was younger, we were very close. He sort of took the place of Dad, and we were happy together. Mom did her best look after us, and she did a good job. She was a good mother and still is. She tried to keep us busy to avoid the hurt for losing our dad. We went to fun places and spent a lot of time outdoors. I was really interested in sports and she saw that Tom and I went to every game we wanted to. We always did lots of camping in the summer too. She also made sure we went to church. We went to Sunday School every week and to other activities in between. We liked it, and other kids' dads took us under their wings. But when I reached my teens, I changed. I wanted to be with friends that thought they were cool but turned out to be terrible. I got involved with a gang and I had a hard time getting out. I kind of fell off the rails then, and it was a long time before I got back on track."

"Well, I'm happy to see that you've changed. How did you meet Charlene? She seems to be such a lovely young woman. I enjoyed spending time with her when we went to the city."

"Well, I won't bore you with the details. I'm ashamed of those years that I spent away from my family. But one day I was in a back alley sitting on an empty barrel, filthy dirty and drinking a bottle of whiskey, and a beautiful young woman walked up to me and said 'Why are you doing that? You're throwing your life away.' I was dumbfounded and didn't know what to say. She just looked me over and at her watch and then said, 'I want to talk with you but not when you're drunk. Clean yourself up and meet me here this time tomorrow for a chat.' I thought she was crazy, and almost told her that, but I was curious. We did meet the next day, and we walked to the nearby park. She had brought a picnic basket and blanket, and we spent most of the day there. It was the beginning of a solid friendship. I haven't had a drink since."

"What a lovely story, Allen! Charlene must be a wonderful woman."

"She's terrific! I've never met another like her. That was over a year ago, and now that we have our child, we think it's time to get married!"

"I'm so happy for you both, Allen. Maybe I can help you with the wedding!"

NINETEEN

Peyton was delighted when Helen showed up at the Lodge. "Just thinking about you all and thought I'd pop in when I was out and about. How are you, my dear?"

Peyton dusted shavings from her clothes and gave the lady a big hug. "I'm great and even happier to see you. What is your 'out and about'?"

"Oh, I had a doctor's appointment. Nothing to worry about, just a check-up. I stopped by our lawyer's office to do some business too. This place looks great! I'd love that tour if it wouldn't interrupt your work too much. Is Tom here? I didn't see his truck."

"Tom isn't here today. I guess he's busy at the log yard."

"Too bad. I don't like to go over there and bother him. It's always so noisy. But I did want to talk to him."

"I can take a break though. I'd love to show you around."

"I'd love that, honey and maybe I'll pop over to your place afterward, Allen. Is Charlene at home today?"

"No, she took the baby to visit friends in the city. She'll be back tomorrow."

Helen looked downcast, not her usual self. "Another day then."

Peyton took her arm and steered her away. "Come

on. Let me show you how beautiful the great room has become. You'll love what we did to the floor. The place is so big, it took the fellow we hired three days to clean and polish it all."

Half an hour later Peyton made coffee and they sat down at the kitchen table. Helen seemed more cheerful and congratulated Peyton for all that she was doing. Peyton protested that it was a team effort and Tom was a big part of it. "We couldn't have come this far if Aunt Julie hadn't introduced Tom to me. He's been a wonderful support to me and everyone else on our team."

"My son is a wonderful man, Peyton. He has a heart for everyone and especially for people who are in need. Ever since he was a small boy, he's loved to help others. Doing chores at home without having to be asked, helping to rake leaves in neighbors' yards, shoveling snow for practically the whole street, carrying people's groceries for them…so much. One day when he was a little boy he said to me, 'I love you so much, Mommy, I'm going to come to your house and shovel your snow whenever you need me to.' Through the years, especially since my husband left us, he's been a big help in our family. That's why he's taken Allen under his wing again after so long.

You know, when he met you here that first night, he liked you right away and mentioned you to me at the Chili Cook-off. I could tell right away that he wanted to know you better, and ever since then he hasn't stop talking about you. It's been such a long time since he had a girlfriend. He went out with a few when he was in high school none of them turn out to be what he wanted. He focused on his love of wood working. That was good, of course, because he studied and worked hard to become the successful businessman that he is. But now the years are going by and I think he's lonely. I see him looking a little sad when he's around the families at our church. He loves children and they love him. It's time he focused on having a partner and a family of his own. I'm surprised and pleased that he's finally interested in someone. I never dreamed that it would be a woman as wonderful as you."

"I haven't had a boyfriend for a long time either, Helen. When I was young, I was shy around everyone, especially boys. I detoured around them and spent a lot of my teen years reading, writing and studying. I got honors in everything I did, but I didn't socialize much with anyone except a few friends at church. In high school I had dates with a couple of guys but they weren't my type. I was busy because I studied to be a Journeyman Carpenter. The high school had classes encouraging that, and on weekends I helped my dad with the construction he was doing to get the hours of experience that was required. When I graduated, I worked at my dad's construction business for a while but then my mom was diagnosed with lung cancer and I spent a lot of time looking after her. So you see, I'm not very experienced with men."

Helen squeezed Payton' hand. "I'm so sorry about your mom. Losing our mothers is the worst thing that happens in our lives. I lost mine many years ago and yet I still think of her all the time. She was a loving mother with a great sense of humor and a love of music, gardening and travelling. And a very good cook! Most of all, she was a devout woman of faith, and she helped us learn to love the Lord. I've tried to raise my boys the way my mother raised us."

"Do you have siblings, Helen?"

"Yes, I do! A sister and a brother. My sister is 82 and my brother is 72. They live far away and we don't see each other much, although we do keep in touch by phone and computer. My dad passed away 25 years ago and my mom the next year."

"Tom is lucky to have you, Helen. I can tell he loves you very much."

"I do. He is so good to me. I don't know what I would do without him." Suddenly Helen's eyes teared up. "Peyton, I came here today to tell Tom something. I wasn't truthful when I said my doctor's appointment was just a check-up. I've been seeing him every couple of weeks for a while. I've been diagnosed with liver cancer."

Peyton was shocked and dismayed. "Helen, that's awful. How long have you known? Does Tom know?"

"No. I didn't want him to get upset about it, since he's so busy, and I didn't know for sure anyway, until today. I have a tumor on my liver and they've done an injection to take a sample. It's cancer alright."

"How big is it? Something that could be removed with surgery?"

"Well, apparently they're not sure if the cancer is isolated or connected with cancer in any other part of the body. They have to do more investigating." She wiped her eyes. "There's a possibility that I might need a transplant."

"I'm so sorry, Helen. You must tell Tom and Allen. You wouldn't want them to find out from someone else. I'm so sorry that I won't be here to help you through this."

"My darling, iIn my heart I was hoping you'd stay here forever. You're exactly the woman that I hoped would be my son's bride. Beautiful, loving, smart and a Child of the King. You know, don't you, that he's already in love with you. He hasn't told me in so many words but I can tell."

Peyton's eyes filled with tears and she reached over to hug Helen. "Actually, I've grown very fond of him too. But neither of us has taken that next step. This place is wonderful, and it's been so delightful to get to know you and your family. But apart from Julie and Ed, our family is just Dad and I, and I really need to go back home. He needs me." She brushed away her tears. "A couple of years ago my mother died of cancer after a terrible year of suffering, and it took both of us a long time to get over it, especially Dad. When she passed, he went into a deep depression and for a long time he wouldn't even leave the house. I had to deal with the business matters myself. I did a few small renos on my own but I was getting desperate, wondering how long we could keep the business going. I told him I wanted to find a job with another company. That kind of snapped him out of it and he has been better since. Thankfully, Aunt Julie & I kept in touch, even though we were many miles away from each other, and when she saw this Lodge for sale, she thought of us. An unusual project but she thought maybe if we could get him interested, it would be just what he needed to get back in tune. It took a lot of persuasion but once he saw it, he gave in. We were both excited and eager to get started and I hoped this renovation would bring him back to what things use to be. It has, somewhat. But now he's having to deal with the accident and a broken leg. I'm afraid that if we don't sell the Lodge quickly, we'll have trouble with the bank and it'll drive him back into depression. I need to be home to help him deal with that. Tom and I both have businesses to look after and we'd be hundreds of miles away from each other. I just don't think it would work for us to get more involved with each other."

God, Helen is so sweet! Please help her through this! I'm sure she would be a wonderful mother-in-law. My mother is in Heaven now. How wonderful it would be to stay here and live the rest of my life with Tom and his family! Why can't I do that, Lord? Dad is going to have Ellie for his life partner. Why can't Tom be mine?

TWENTY

Sunday morning came and Tom arrived to pick up Peyton. She was a bit nervous since she hadn't been in a church for several years. The small church was very pretty and surrounded with lovely trees and flowers. It was a beautiful morning and the door was open, with Pastor Alex welcoming folks as they entered. Tom introduced Peyton to him and he was intrigued to hear she was working on the Lodge project. "I'm delighted that it's going to be renovated and opened again. It used to be one of the most important landmarks of our town. I hope you will feel free to join us every Sunday while you're here."

"Thank you, sir. You're welcome to drop by the site and see what's been done so far. A few more weeks and the Lodge will be finished and put up for sale."

Allen and Charlene waved as they had saved spots for them to sit together. As Tom and Peyton walked through the church, she could see heads turning to see who was with Tom. They sat at one end of the pew and Charlene slid over to them with the baby. "Don't be nervous. I was in the same boat when I first came with Allen. These folks are nosy but very friendly."

Helen waved to them from the center where she was sitting with friends. Peyton recognized Jason sitting on the other side of the church with a couple she assumed were his parents. After the service she would try to connect with them but now the musicians were tuning up on the platform and people were taking their seats.

Tom put his Bible down and went to chat with a few folks nearby, then came back as the music started. Peyton was pleasantly surprised at how nice the service was. She found that she could sing along with a few of the hymns she remembered from the past, and Tom was impressed. When it was time for the Scripture reading, Tom took his Bible and went up to the front to read a passage. The portion chosen was very fitting for what was happening in Dave's life and in Helen's.

"Our reading today is from 2 Corinthians 12:7-10, written by Paul the Apostle, who was suffering from a "thorn in the flesh", as he called it. We don't actual know what that was, but here's what he says about it. *"One of Satan's angels was sent to make me suffer terribly, so I would not feel too proud. Three times I begged the Lord to make this suffering go away. But He replied, 'My kindness is all you need. My power is strongest when you are weak. So if Christ keeps giving me His power, I will gladly brag about how weak I am. Yes, I am glad to be weak or insulted or mistreated or to have troubles and sufferings if it is for Christ. Because when I am weak, I am strong."*

(Contemporary English Version)

Peyton looked over to Helen, who met her eyes and smiled. Pastor Alex returned to the pulpit. "Thank you, Tom. Those are beautiful words for us. We all will experience some burdens in our lives, it's inevitable. But God has a plan for each one of us, and He allows things to happen for a reason. He will be there for us, no matter where or when."

When Tom sat down again, Peyton reached for his hand and smiled at him. Coming to church, and seeing him reading from God's Word, was a blessing. She felt like her heart was opening for the Lord and for him. Seeing him in those moments of faith was helping to put her on track again. And her feelings for Tom were becoming stronger and she couldn't stop them.

Pastor Alex continued the service and afterwards announced that coffee and snacks were available to everyone downstairs. Tom took Peyton to speak with Jason and his family. Peyton was interested to hear Jake and Anna Taylor were owners of the nice café that she'd been in. Jason stood around for few minutes to be polite but after greeting Tom and Peyton, his parents gave him permission to spend the afternoon with his friends. Peyton and Tom sat with the Taylors and talked about the renovation site. They seemed happy to have their son working there.

"We want to thank you both for giving Jason this opportunity. For a while after he went to court, he was very sullen about the Judge's order to work off all those hours." Anna was teary. "The Judge stipulated that he was not to have anything to do with those teens he was involved with but it's been hard for him. Three months is a long time for a boy his age, and we've been worried. We're scared he'll go back to them."

Tom sympathized. "Yeah, me too. But giving him somewhere to go after school, being around adults who give him legitimate work to do and praise when he does a good job – that's just what he needs."

"It sure is working. Now that he's doing landscaping,

he's really happy. Talks about it all the time at home. He'd like to take some classes outside of school as well, and when he graduates, he wants to study Horticulture and Landscape Design."

Peyton was delighted. "That's wonderful! We're really pleased to have him working with us. He tells me that he's almost completed his court order. Let me know when it's finished and I'll put him on the payroll. It may not be for long though, since we only have a few weeks left."

TWENTY-ONE

After her first week of work at the motel, Tracey was exhausted but also proud of herself. For the first few days she'd struggled because she'd never learned how to do the kind of work that was expected. Her parents were wealthy and hired other people to look after their home and their daughter. When she was in school, she'd taken a class in home economics but didn't like it much, as it was mostly about learning to cook, sew, clean and manage a home, none of which appealed to a young rich girl. Now she was learning how to do real housework. This past week she had managed to make friends with the other chambermaids and they were happy to teach her, probably because it would take a load off them. She resolved to work as hard as she could because her future was unsure. She knew Andre was keeping his eye on her and she wanted to show him that she was willing to work.

This morning, while she and another woman were folding sheets in the laundry, Andre appeared. "Good morning, ladies. What a beautiful day outside! Sandy, why don't you take a break and I'll finish this up with Tracey." When the door closed behind her, Andre smiled at Tracey. "Well, you've done very well this week. What do you think of the job? Is it something you want to continue with?"

"Actually, I like it. It's not as hard as I thought it

would be. The staff have been very friendly and helpful and I think I'm getting the hang of it. It feels good to do something worthwhile. Yes, I would like to keep the job."

"Okay. I'm willing to put you on the payroll starting today." He took an envelope out of his pocket and passed it to her. "Payday here is every two weeks but I know you need the money now, so here's a week's pay for what you've done this week. You can live here for a while longer, but it can't be for too long. My crew will be wondering why you're living here and getting paid for it too. Besides, I'm going to need the room soon, because summer is coming and we get really busy with tourists. Any word from your parents?"

"Nothing. I tried many times to get them on my phone but it always goes to voicemail. I don't think they're in the country anyway."

"Well, ask around and see if you can find an apartment. Make sure it's in a good neighborhood, though. I'll talk to Tom and see if he knows of one. If you find something, let me know. I don't mind helping you with the rent money until you can afford to pay it yourself."

Tracey was amazed. "Why would you do all this for me, Andre? You hardly know me."

"Because you need it, I guess. Tom told me about your parents locking you out and I can sympathize. When I was younger, I was in a similar situation, only I was a foster kid with people who didn't like me and only wanted the money. When I turned eighteen, and my foster parents weren't getting any more money for me, I had to go on my own. Back then, after a teen reached that age, the government didn't provide anything for kids like us. We were on our own. At first it was scary but Tom and his mom took me in for a while. He helped me find a place to live and gave me a job at the log home site. We became good friends and I worked there for six years. He encouraged me to do a lot of things, including buying this motel. I wouldn't be as successful as I am now if not for him. I'm very grateful to have him as my friend and I try to be as good a man as he is. For you, I'm paying it forward."

TWENTY-TWO

The time finally came for the Lodge to be put up for sale. Julie called Peyton to ask if she and Ed could bring over some furniture and other things to use for staging of upcoming showings. Staging would help sell the Lodge faster and possibly increase the amount buyers would be willing to pay. People liked to imagine themselves in the various rooms. Mentally moving in, Julie called it, and she was an expert at it.

"Please do, come on over! I'd love to see you. We haven't heard from you for ages!"

Julie laughed. "You're right. The last few weeks have been great for Ed and I. We've sold three homes, each one in a different location! I don't know how that happens but every so often it does. We've been busy alright. But I'm not complaining." Ed's truck arrived, with Julie's car behind, and he and some helpers began unloading. Because the Lodge was so large and advertised as a hotel, it was going to be a bit hard to stage. Julie chose to do four areas: the great room with the dining area and large fireplace, the newly renovated kitchen, two second-floor bedrooms, and the master suite on the top floor. Once unloaded, Ed took his crew upstairs to put the beds together. In the great room, the previous owners had left some nice dining tables and chairs, so Julie and Peyton began polishing and decorating the tables with several settings of china that Julie had brought from home. They also brought in several other things – bowls of artificial fruit, a few house plants, coffee tables, flowers and lamps, toiletry items and towels for the bathrooms, and pillows and bedding for the two upstairs rooms.

The emphasis today was to clean each area before putting things in place. Peyton called Jason to see if he'd like to work, since it was a Saturday, and he was glad to help. Surprisingly, when he and his parents arrived, they didn't just drop him off as they usually did. They all got out, with Anna carrying a big box of donuts.

"We heard that you were staging today and thought you might appreciate some extra help. Just to thank you for helping Jason so much. The goodies are for everyone. Please help yourself."

Peyton was very appreciative and insisted that everyone sit down around a table and have a coffee and donut right away. They got to talking, and Jake and Anna told them they had lived in Rocky View for many years. Anna worked as a waitress and Jake drove semitrucks back and forth from Canada to Alaska. Sometimes Anna went with him and helped to drive, since she had a commercial license too and loved to travel. When the Lodge opened for business, she was hired as desk clerk and hostess. At forty-five years of age, she surprised everyone when she became pregnant with Jason. Once he was born, neither one of them wanted to go on the road anymore so they settled down in Rocky View for good. Jake took a job at Tom's lumber yard and still worked there.

Peyton wanted to know the history of the Lodge and Jake was pleased to share. "It was built many years ago by a wealthy American man who owned the property, which is actually quite large and fairly close to the National Park gates. The land had never been developed and for years was untouched, but then a village started growing up near-by. Homes and stores were being built and he decided to get in on it. He built several businesses and then sold them to the locals. Some of them are still operating - the bar, our grocery store, the clothing stores, the barber and our coffee shop & bakery. Eventually he called in men and machines to clear some of his land to make a subdivision, which is what we're in right now - Mountainview Estates. And he built the best one – the Lodge."

"It took him three years to finish it though." Anna sighed. "Apparently medical issues slowed him down… he had a heart condition himself and he lost his wife to cancer…but eventually he was able to finish. There was a Grand Opening and the Lodge became noted as the most beautiful building in area. It was built to be an option for families who couldn't afford the expensive lodging in the Park. They would be able to get cheaper rates staying outside the gates and doing day trips instead. And it was very successful. Loads of tourists came, summer and winter, and in slow seasons we locals used the great room for events. The owner made a lot of money and everyone loved the place."

"So why did it shut down then? It seems to be in relatively good condition overall and still very luxurious."

"Well, nobody around here seems to know. The Lodge had been doing well, as far as we knew, for more than twenty years. Every so often the owner would come up from the States and inspect the place but the staff hardly ever saw him. Everything was done through the manager, who lived off site. Then one day a sign was put up on the door that it had closed down. No advance notices for staff, or opportunities to discuss it. Some people think that the owner, who hadn't been seen for a long time, had finally passed away. Others think the manager had a battle with the owner and got fired. Either way, he just left it and didn't even tell anyone. Eventually it was sold to a woman who lived in the States but she never moved in. She hired Julie to look after the building for a couple of years and it was finally put it up for sale again. And you bought it!"

"Wow! What a story. Sounds like you loved working here, did you Anna?"

"I did. And I wouldn't mind taking the job again when the Lodge opens again. I love meeting people from all over the world and helping them have a great holiday."

"Well, we'll be advertising the Lodge as doing just that. Time will tell. We'll be sure to let you know what happens."

TWENTY-THREE

All three Taylors worked hard cleaning and painting and stayed until the late afternoon. Tom had come at lunchtime with sandwiches and drinks for everyone, then pick up a brush and stayed to help as well. He had done a great job staining and installing the kitchen cupboards, and had also made a beautiful island with drawers and cupboards underneath, all with reclaimed lumber. The commercial equipment had finally arrived and was put in place - double sinks with gooseneck and wall mounted faucets, a large dishwasher and a rack oven that could hold up to 30 pans. The old appliances had been replaced with a top-grade stove and refrigerator.

Just as things were winding down, Julie arrived with some news. She'd been having coffee with a client at the café when she overheard something that made her skin crawl. A young woman was eating at the counter and a man at the other end was talking to her about the Subaru vehicle outside. "He asked if it was hers and she said yes. He said it was too bad about the big scrape along the side. The woman replied that it had happened when she was moving and she hadn't had time to get it fixed."

Peyton and Tom looked at each other. "So? Why is that news?"

Julie was excited. "There's more! A car and a pick-up, both coming here from the city, a deer running across the highway in front of them, and a driver who wouldn't move over. The woman was scornful, blaming the truck driver, complaining he was responsible for the damage to her car. Doesn't that ring a bell?"

Peyton heart skipped a beat, but she had to be reasonable. "There are so many people and so many highways in this province…how could you possibly know who she was talking about?"

Julie shrugged. "I couldn't help myself. I went over to them and asked about it, pretending to take her side of what happened. Found out that it was the same day and in the same area as Dave's accident."

"Wow! What a coincidence. But we don't even know what that other vehicle looked like."

"I do. That's why when she left the café, I ran after her, pretending she'd left a glove. She said it wasn't hers but thanked me. I told her my name and asked for hers, welcoming her to town. She said she'd grown up here but had lived in the city for several years and was now moving back. And when she drove away, I took a picture of her car and the license plate. Here, take a look."

The car in Julie's photo was a black Mercedes-Benz SUV. It did have a big scrape along the passenger side. And Julie had heard the driver's name -Tracey.

Tom was dumbfounded. He'd seen Tracey's Subaru around town a couple of times since she came back, but not close enough to notice any damage. Peyton felt sick, thinking that this woman might have been responsible for her dad's troubles. "I need to call Dad to get the names of the people who stopped for him. They would know more."

Tom was cautious about it. "Didn't you tell me that Dave had already been contacted by the RCMP about it? I think you should let them handle it. Let's call your dad first and see what he thinks."

TWENTY-FOUR

The next two weeks went by quickly. Everything in the Lodge was completed and the place was ready for the showing. Julie had contacted other realtors in the province, inviting them to come and see the Lodge. She was proud that the place looked beautiful, but also sad to think of what was coming next. Peyton looked so much like her deceased mother, and the time spent with her brought back memories. Julie loved having so much time with her niece, but selling the Lodge meant they would soon be parting.

Tom was gloomy too. He and Peyton had talked to Dave online about what Julie had discovered. It was up to Dave whether or not he wanted to pass the information along to the RCMP. Dave was reluctant. It didn't really matter to him who was driving the car that night. He had no evidence. His truck was insured, and as far as they were concerned, it was a write-off. His pick-up was old anyway and he would just have to take what they gave him. If in fact Tracey was the driver of that other vehicle, stirring up the waters would probably result in Dave having to lay charges against her. Then the woman might charge him for damages to her very expensive car, and they both would end up in court. As for Dave's medical issue, his health insurance was covering everything.

Peyton was fuming and tried to persuade her father to get more information, possibly from the young couple that stopped for Dave. But he refused. He was tired of it all and just wanted to leave things be. Tom agreed with Dave, but Peyton was angry. She glared at Tom, accusing that he only said that because Tracey was his ex-girlfriend. When he protested, she stomped out of the room and slammed the door, leaving Tom to say goodbye. Dave smiled. "Don't worry, Tom. She'll get over it. I'm doing the right thing."

The date for Allen and Charlene's wedding had been set, and their parents were busy making sure it would be wonderful. Charlene's parents had arrived from the east, bringing with them her grandmother's wedding dress. Cleaned and with a bit of fitting, it was beautiful. Helen offered her a lovely lace veil that she had worn for her wedding many years ago. Allen managed to locate and refresh the suit he had worn on his graduation day.

Tom and Peyton were avoiding each other, even though she was the Maid of Honor and he Allen's Best Man. Peyton was still annoyed that Tom had agreed with Dave about the accident, although she had to admit that they were right. Now she was flustered because she didn't have a fancy dress for the wedding. Helen invited her to come for tea and look through a closet full of her dresses, not worn for years but still in good condition.

"Thanks for having me over, Helen. I really need a break from the Lodge today. Julie is having showings with several other realtors in the area, and I don't want to be around."

"Wouldn't you want to be there to take credit for your hard work?"

"No, I don't want listen to people's remarks, good or

bad. I love the Lodge and this area so much, and it makes me sad to realize that I'm going to leave soon."

"I'm very sad about that too, my dear. We've all come to love you, including my son, who is very moody about it these days. Have you thought about a life with Tom? He loves you and I know it."

"We've talked about it, Helen. We both have feelings about each other. But there's nothing I can do. I have no choice except to return to the city. We have a temporary mortgage with the bank, and we have to take care of it soon or we'll lose all our other customers. And because Dave can't work right now, it's up to me. We might lose our business completely if I don't go back."

Helen tried on several dresses and they were all very nice. But not quite what she wanted. Finally she found the one she liked best – a sleeveless floor length lavender floral print. When she tried it on, it was a perfect fit. "You look absolutely stunning, sweetheart. You know what? This is my favorite too. Please wear it for the wedding and then take it home with you. It is my gift to you and I want you to remember this moment."

Because of the number of folks that ended up being invited, the wedding was moved to the church, which was better anyway for the those that were helping with the reception. The ceremony was beautiful and went off without a hitch. Charlene's mother Anita came down the aisle on the arm of their friend Andre. Once she was seated, Best Man Tom and Maid of Honor Peyton did the same, then took their places on either side of the bride and groom. Then the traditional music began and everyone turned to watch Charlene's father Scott walk his lovely daughter down the aisle. Allen was almost tearing up as he took her hand and helped her into place. Tom did his part of the ceremony but couldn't stop watching

Peyton, she looked so beautiful. Once everyone was in place, their eyes met and she managed a tiny smile.

Pastor Alex had known Helen's family for many years and was pleased to be asked to do the ceremony. He was aware of Allen's past and was so pleased to know that he was finally settled and starting a family. "Welcome family, friends and loved ones. We are gathered today to celebrate the union of Allen McCauley and Charlene Smithers. We are here to support them in their commitment of love, and to share their joy as they choose to spend their lives together." He raised his eyes and for some reason his attention was drawn to the back of the room. A man with a hood over his head was standing there.

For a moment, the pastor was a bit rattled but then continued. "Allen and Charlene, your marriage will be a lifelong promise to love, respect and honor each other through the good, the bad and the unexpected." Pastor Alex had done so many wedding ceremonies over the years that he could do them by heart and that was a good thing today. He was able to continue, with the couple exchanging their vows and rings, followed by a prayer and the final announcement, 'You may kiss your Bride.' It was difficult for him to be himself, congratulating the bride and groom and their parents and chatting with others milling around in the foyer. Because the man watching from the back corner was Tom and Allen's father.

The ceremony was over and the reception a success. Tom was happy for his brother but wished he was the groom. How strange it seemed for Allen to marry before he did! His little brother now had a wife and child. Tom was thirty and an uncle. Weren't most men married by now or at least in a solid relationship?

As boys, they had been very close, even more so after

their dad left. But when Allen became a teenager, things changed and Tom was the stern father figure who had to make sure his boy was behaving. It was difficult for them both. Tom blamed himself when Allen stayed away from home for days at a time. He suspected the boy was involved with some sort of gang and using drugs, and he didn't know how to stop it. Their relationship took a nose-dive and for the past years they had no contact with each other at all. Thankfully, Allen was so blessed to meet Charlene. She was his lifeline to something better.

Tom agreed that it was a lovely ceremony and reception. He stayed to do the cleaning up and recruited Jason and a couple of his friends to help, promising to play some basketball with them afterwards. Helen and the other ladies had gone home. They had worked so hard to make the event successful, they deserved the break. Charlene's parents were busy arranging to spend a week in the National Park, and Helen offered to look after Jasmine so Allen and Charlene could enjoy a honeymoon. They had not decided where, but with a couple of weeks off work and no baby to look after, anything would be a wonderful break.

When things were finally cleaned up and the chairs and tables stowed away, Tom and the boys had a quick game. He and Jason were just closing up when Pastor Alex came by. Jason said goodnight and left to walk home, as he lived nearby. "Do you have a few minutes, Tom? I've got a coffee machine in my office. I'd like to chat with you."

Settled in his office, the coffee was a boost for the hard work they both had been doing. "That was a lovely ceremony, Pastor. You did a good job."

"Thanks. You too, Best Man. You and Peyton looked superb walking down the aisle. I've been told that you two are very good friends. Maybe I'll be asked to do something like this for you soon?"

"I wish! I like her very much but I'm afraid she's not meant for me. In a short time she'll be going back to her city life."

"Sorry to hear that. I've noticed how you look at each other, though. There's definitely something between you. She seems to be very sweet. Helen sure loves her."

"Mom has a knack for matchmaking, that's true. She's told me that she wants Peyton and I to marry. But I don't want her pushing me to do anything."

"Have you prayed about it, Tom? I remember you saying a few years ago that you believed God had a plan for you. If you and Peyton are meant to be together, He will make it happen in His time. Don't give up!

Anyway, I asked you to stay because I have something else to tell you. Did you notice that I fumbled a bit when I was speaking? I want to tell you why. I saw someone, a man with a hood in the foyer, peeking in to see but not be seen."

"Really? I didn't notice. Maybe it was a photographer. Or someone who was coming in late?"

"No, it wasn't. He must have slipped into the church and hidden until everyone went into the sanctuary. As soon as the ceremony started, he snuck in to watch. I saw him from the pulpit, just for a moment, but enough to recognize him. Tom, it was your dad."

TWENTY-FIVE

Tom was dumbfounded. "That can't be true. It must have been someone else. I never saw him in the foyer. No one did or they would have told us by now."

"He probably watched until the ceremony was over, and Allen and Charlene started coming back up the aisle, then slipped out the back door. The man was definitely Peter, Tom, and he knew that I'd seen him. He's back in town."

Tom felt sick. Was it really his dad? It was 18 years since Peter had left the family. Why would he show up now? Anger surged up in Tom. Why would they even want to see him? Should he tell Allen and Helen that he was here? What would happen if he told them now? Allen and Charlene are just married and expecting a wonderful honeymoon. He didn't want to spoil their happiness. If he told Helen, could she take the shock of having her husband show up at this point in their lives?

Pastor Alex waited for the reaction, then gently spoke. "Your dad must have found out somehow that Allen was getting married today, maybe from someone who's been in touch with him over the years. Do you think your mother knows?"

"I don't know. I don't think she would keep that from us, but maybe. She knows how I feel. He hurt us all so much that I've hated him for years. Coming face to face with him again would be very hard to do. I'm afraid it wouldn't be a good idea."

"Perhaps that's what you both need, Tom. A time to come together, face to face with what he did, and hear him apologize. I'm sure he regrets what he did to your family or he wouldn't have come to the church today. He wanted to see you all."

Tom sighed. "If that's all he wanted, he's probably left town by now. I hope so. I don't want Mom to get upset."

"If Helen doesn't know about this right now, and she finds out that you didn't tell her, she will be very angry with you. If I were you, I would tell her and Allen as soon as you can. Word gets around quickly in a small town like this. Just seeing his truck somewhere could start the rumors. I think Helen and Allen should be told as soon as possible."

Later that evening Tom called Allen and Helen and asked if they could meet at her house. She was at home relaxing after the busy wedding day, and Allen was a bit annoyed to be asked on such a night. But Tom said it was important for them to get together before the couple left for their honeymoon. He promised them it wouldn't take long. Pastor Alex had offered to attend but Tom thought it better to just have the family.

When Tom broke the news about Peter, he was surprised at the response. Helen already knew that Peter was in town. In fact, he had met her at the store that morning and had talked briefly with her. She had lost her love for the man long ago but understood him wanting to see his son's wedding. She didn't want him to be seen, so she had suggested he just slip in and out afterward. "I didn't want to tell you boys and spoil this day for you. But

Pastor Alex recognized him and we had to tell you before the word gets around."

"What are we supposed to do? Get all excited because Daddy's back after 18 years?" Allen was angry. "I thought he was dead, otherwise he would have come back to us long ago."

"Where has he been for all those years, Mom? Has he told you?" Tom was hurting too. "He owes us an answer and an apology."

"Yes, he does. That's why I asked him to come over. He's waiting for me to call him. When you were young, you wouldn't have understood. I didn't, at the time. But now I'd like to hear what he has to say too. Are you willing to talk with him?"

Tom and Allen looked at each other and shrugged. Helen took out her cell phone and dialed a number. "He's here. I'll unlock the back door for you."

Peter must have been waiting outside because in just minutes he rapped on the door. Tom went to answer and not a word was said, just a gesture toward the staircase. At the top of the stairs, Barkley greeted them excitedly and Helen scooped him up. The Shih Tzu's enthusiasm broke the ice and Peter took the offered mug of coffee.

Peter looked the same as when he'd left, although there were wrinkles and gray hairs, and more around the waist. Helen tried to get some conversation going, mentioning how nice the wedding had been and enquiring about Allen's intentions for a honeymoon. No one wanted small talk, though. After a few minutes, Tom steered to the reason they were there.

"Dad, how about if we talk about a day 18 years ago. It's something that we've never understood and it's time we got some answers. Allen and I went off to school that morning like we always did and when we came home,

Mom's life had been shattered and our family changed forever. We want to hear what you did that day and why."

Peter sighed and took a moment to compose himself. "I know you all hate me for what I did and I admit it was a horrible thing. I have no excuse for being such a coward. I cheated on you, Helen. I'm so sorry! For years I was travelling and working away from home, meeting other people...I was so lonely. I should have found a better job so I could be with my family. Instead, I developed a friendship with another woman. She was a single parent with two young children. I knew it was the wrong thing to do, but we became good friends and I loved the children. Eventually she and I fell in love. I tried to hide the relationship from you by sending money and gifts, lying to you about why I had to be away all the time. But it got harder and harder to do that, and then one day my friend announced that she was pregnant. Then I had to look after two families. I tried for a while but I just couldn't do it anymore."

"You chose them over us, is that it?" Allen was fuming. "When you left, you couldn't even say goodbye! I remember the day when Tom and I came home and saw Mom at the kitchen table, in tears. All she told us then was that you were moving away. We thought you meant just for a while but not forever."

"I had to, son. I can't tell you how many nights I lay in bed, thinking about you boys and the good times we had. And wishing we all were together, Helen. If only I had stopped things before they got to that level, but I didn't."

"Does this other woman know about us? Did you divorce Mom and not tell us?"

"The other woman never knew about you. She was divorced from her ex and didn't want to marry again. I lied and told her I was divorced too. And I was, I guess, in a way."

Helen spoke up. "Peter and I have never been legally divorced. We have what they call a Judicial Separation. It's a legal separation of spouses that doesn't dissolve the marriage bond. We signed the papers a few years after we parted. I didn't tell you two because I didn't want to stir up things again."

Tom shook his head. "You helped raise three other children, Dad? How old would they be now? And where do you live?"

"The boys are both studying at the university in Calgary. My daughter is 16 and we live in the National Park. We both have jobs there."

"Does your other family know that you're here today?"

His eyes moistened. "No. My partner battled leukemia for the last five years and finally passed a few months ago. They don't know about you at all. Something I have to get up the nerve to tell them."

What more could be said? Tom felt sad that their father had not been in touch with them for the last eighteen years, and he was hurt that Helen had kept so much from them. It was obvious that Helen and Peter had seen each other over the years if they had a legal separation at some point in time. Why hadn't they let their sons know that? They had no idea where their dad was, or whether he was even alive. Finding out their father was having an affair with another woman would have been hard to take, but they would have gotten over it eventually. But the way he did it was so hurtful, disappearing without telling them and never having contact with them for so many years. Now Helen must have told Peter that Allen was getting married. Pastor Alex had encouraged Tom to arrange this meeting but if not for him, Peter would probably have disappeared again. Tom felt disgusted. Peter was not the father that they'd loved so long ago.

TWENTY-SIX

Tracey was enjoying her work at the motel. She was glad to have some income but it was more than that. She felt like a new person, being part of a team and friends with the other employees, who were all older than her. They inspired her to work hard. It was a small motel and there wasn't a lot of pressure on them. The past few weeks she'd worked both day and night shifts and enjoyed both. And Andre was more than a good boss. She felt he was becoming more like a friend. She liked him more every day.

That morning, Andre had news for her. One of his neighbors had sold his home and the new owner wanted to rent out the basement suite. "Are you still looking for a place, Tracey? Our neighborhood is fairly new, three or four years old, and a lot of the homes on that street have basement suites. I haven't been in that one but I'm sure it's nice. Would you like to take a look at it after work today?"

Tracey was surprised but excited. "That would be great, Andre! Thank you!"

At the end of her shift, Andre was waiting outside. "We can take my car. I probably know the route through town better than you. What brought you here, Tracey? Tom told me that you were living in the city for years."

"Rocky View was my hometown until I graduated

and moved with my parents to Calgary. I loved the city and still do, but now it's way too expensive for me to live there. My life has changed a lot, especially recently, and times are difficult. I remembered my childhood days here and decided to start over."

"Wow! What did your parents think of that?"

"My parents are wealthy and life in the city was wonderful while it lasted. But over time, two relationships failed, and the trust fund that my grandparents gave me dried up. I got fed up with city life and with my parents, who had supported me in the past but then abandoned me.

To be truthful, I was hoping to connect with Tom again. We were high school sweethearts, you know, until we graduated. When my parents moved us to the city Tom and I lost contact. I had hoped that he and I would someday marry, but instead we went our separate ways. Two years later I married someone else, but it only lasted for a couple of years. I moved back in with my parents for a while but they weren't happy with that. They are very affluent but they wanted me to get a job and move out on my own. I'd never done anything like that in my life. Long story short, they kicked me out! I couldn't live in the big city on my own, with no income. All I could think of to do was come back home and start my life over."

"That must have been very hard for you. Do you intend to keep in touch with your parents? Do they know that you're here now?"

"I don't know. They haven't contacted me for over a year. They do a lot of business overseas and I don't think they even care where I am."

"I'm sorry about that, Tracey. When was your trip here? The weather last month was pretty awful. Some days, not a good time to be driving."

"It was the 29th of May. And yes, it was awful. I loaded

up my car with as much of my belongings as I could fit in, probably too much, because I could hardly see out the back window. I'd spent the whole morning packing and didn't leave the city until early afternoon. I was tired but excited that I was finally on my way. But it started to rain almost immediately. By evening it was very dark, still raining, and I was only halfway here. I was having trouble seeing the road and I thought I'd better stop someplace to spend the night, even if I had to sleep in the car. That's when I had the accident."

"What happened? Was it serious? Your car only has a few scrapes on it."

"I had caught up to a pickup truck and he was driving slowly so I pulled out to pass. But before I could get back, a deer jumped across in front of us. I swerved and hit the truck but not that hard. I was able to steer back on the road."

"Wow! I bet that scared you."

"I was pretty rattled. It must have been okay though, because when I looked for the truck, he must have gone by. The weather was so awful, I just kept going. When I stopped at the next gas station, I saw the damage and felt terrible. I looked for the pickup but it wasn't there. And I had no idea who the driver was. No one has contacted me since then, so I guess it turned out okay. I'll have to get my car fixed eventually, but it isn't a high priority for me right now."

Andre and Tracey took the tour of the basement suite and she was delighted. It was very modern, two bedrooms with a nice living room area and kitchenette. The previous tenant had left a few pieces of furniture, a bit old but she was glad to have them. The owner mentioned that there was a thrift store nearby if she needed other items. Andre pointed out that the area was close to a Walmart and other businesses and bus stops. He was able to persuade the owner to let her rent the place for a very reasonable price. This would be the first time she'd ever had her own home! She couldn't ask for more.

"Thank you so much, Andre! You've been so kind to me over the last few weeks. And finding this apartment for me is amazing! It means a new life for me. I don't know how to thank you."

"You just did, Tracey." He smiled and his eyes connected with hers. "I appreciate the good job you've done so far at the motel and will keep doing. It helps my business and that's all I need."

TWENTY-SEVEN

Peyton hadn't talked with Dave for a couple of weeks. Now that Julie was showing the completed renos, they should be discussing the financial aspects of their flip. It was possible any day now that they would get an offer on the lodge. Today she was zoom-talking with Dave and Julie, figuring out how much the renovations had cost and what price they should put on the lodge in order to make a reasonable profit. Initially, they had purchased the lodge for $350,000 and Julie was suggesting that they put the newly completed lodge up for sale at $600,000.

Dave thought differently. "Initially we paid $350,000 to buy the lodge and now we owe another $250,000 for the renovation expenses. So that's $600,000 right there. We would need at least another $150,000 as our profit to continue with our business. So let me suggest this: let's start with the price of $900,000 and see how it goes. Think of all the lodge has to offer! Six guest bedrooms, all with ensuite bathrooms, and a master suite with an ensuite as well in the loft. And a commercial kitchen, utility rooms and main floor washrooms, and a communal lounge and dining area. Almost everything inside has been remodeled and the landscaping is amazing! I think we could easily sell the place for more because it's now a high-grade hotel. As beautiful as it is, with the location so close to the National Park, it will likely draw in lots of guests. That means a huge cash flow, summer and winter! The new owners will need to do a lot of advertising, of course, because it hasn't been open for several years. But they'll have no problem doing that. "

Julie was excited. "What do you think, Peyton?"

"I think he's right. Start with a higher price so we have room for negotiation. Go for it, Julie!"

Dave was pleased. "Thanks, Julie. And I'm so proud of you, Peyton. You've done a wonderful job with the lodge and made this flip the best we've ever done. I couldn't have done it any better if I'd had been there."

Julia promised to contact other realtors with the suggested sale price and thanked Dave & Peyton for the opportunity. She closed off the conversation happily looking forward to a significant commission.

Dave wanted to talk with Peyton privately. "Honey, I'm so happy that this has turned out so well for us."

"Thanks, Dad. It's been wonderful to do the flip in such a beautiful setting, with this nice little town nearby. The locals we've hired have been such hard workers. Not only that, they have become my friends and I'm so grateful. I'm going to miss them. And we need to give a lot of credit to Tom. We couldn't have done it at all without his help."

"You know what, kiddo? I'd like to see your masterpiece now that it's complete. Ellie and I have been talking about going to see you again."

"That would be nice. Is she able to take the time off?"

"She's going to retire in a few months and she has a lot of vacation time she needs to use up before then." He paused. "I've made a decision, honey. I'm going to retire too. No more flips."

Peyton was dismayed. "Dad, is it because of your health? Is there something you haven't told me?"

"No, Kitten. In fact, I feel better than I've felt for a long time. I just think it's time for me to put the past behind me and open a new chapter in my life. And I think you should do that too."

"What about our business? Where does that leave us?"

"I've been considering that and I have some plans that I'd like to talk to you about. As soon as possible. This week if works for you."

"Of course, Dad. I'll be happy to see you."

"There's something else I want you to know and get your mind around. Ellie and I are in love and we want to spend the rest of our lives with each other. We're planning to get married soon."

"Wow! That is something, Dad! Although I'm not totally surprised. I saw how you looked at each other when we were with you last time. I've come to grips with that since then, and I believe that Mom would have wanted you to be happy. Congrats to you both, Dad."

"Thank you, sweetie. We'll talk more about everything when we come. Wednesday then? See you then!"

Peyton's mind whirled. The news of Dave's retirement shocked her. In her mind he wasn't old enough to retire! And having a new life with Ellie? She was a nice woman, granted. But would she come and live in their family home? She didn't like the idea of living with her dad and Ellie. Three's a crowd. Where would that put her?

The idea of going back to her city home was scary. If Dave moved in with Ellie, he would want to sell their home. She couldn't afford to keep up large home on her own, so she would have to find someplace else to live. And she would also have to find a new job. She couldn't continue their business on her own. Not in a big city. The hardest thought was losing contact with her friends in Rocky View. But it appeared that the time had come. She was suddenly tearful and aching to be with him. The truth was plain. She loved him and had for a long time.

TWENTY-EIGHT

After dropping Tracey back at the motel, Andre drove across town to see Tom. He was feeling uneasy about what Tracey had told him and wanted Tom's opinion. He seemed to recall that Peyton's dad had been in similar accident a while ago. Could Tracey have been the cause of Dave's accident and subsequent medical problems? He hoped not. He was beginning to feel something for her and he didn't want anything to spoil it.

Tom was getting out of his truck when Andre pulled into the yard. The men had been good friends for years and were happy to see each other. Andre loved Carver too and it was mutual. The dog practically knocked him over when he came running. "Hi there, buddy! Such a good boy!"

"Hey, man!" They shook hands. "How are you, Andre? Good to see you. It's been a while."

"Yes, I've been pretty busy at the motel. Starting to get more tourists these last few weeks, which is good! I can't complain. How are you doing?"

"Fine! Back to normal now that all our crew members are back at work. For a while there, some of them spent a lot of time helping Peyton out at the lodge. But the renos are finished now, I think. The place is up for sale."

"Yes, I noticed the realtor's sign at the turn-off. What's happening with you and Peyton now?"

"What do you mean? Nothing's happening. Who told you there was?"

"Everyone in town knows that you have a new girlfriend."

"Well, you can tell them to forget about her because she'll be leaving town soon. Her home is in Calgary and she'll be going back there once the project is finished. Which is very soon."

"Well, if I were you, I'd be working hard to stop her. It's obvious that you two are in love. You just don't realize it. She's worth fighting for."

"Is that the reason you stopped in today? To give me advice?"

"Well, yes and no. I came to talk with you about Tracey."

"What about her, Andre? I haven't seen her around for a while. It was good of you to give her a job."

"Actually, I'm very glad I hired her. She's reliable and works hard, and her co-workers really like her. She's got a good sense of humor too. But there's something about her that disturbs me. It's her car, that has been sitting in my parking lot for the last few couple of months."

"What about it? I told her she could park it there. Do you need the space for customers now?"

"Well, we're not that busy yet but we will be soon. But that's not what I'm worried about. Did you hear about the accident that Peyton's dad was involved in a while ago? He was driven off the road by another vehicle and he ended up in a ditch against a tree."

"Peyton told me about that. Her dad broke his leg in two places and has been laid up for quite some time.

That's why I've been helping her with renovations of the Lodge. Her dad hasn't been able to work ever since."

"The thing that bothers me is that it was a hit and run. And I think the other driver might have been Tracey."

"What?" Tom was aghast. "Seriously? What makes you think that?"

"I've been trying to find an apartment for her and I finally did. She's been staying at the motel for the last couple of weeks and she couldn't stay forever, so I told her I would help her find a place somewhere. I had been trying, with not much luck because it's not easy in this town. But the other day, just up the street from my place, I saw some people moving in so I walked over for a chat. It so happens that they have a basement suite they want to rent out. I took Tracey over there today to have a look and she really likes it. The owners were glad to find a tenant so quickly."

"I'm happy to hear that, Andre. She was having a tough time until she moved back here. It's good that she's finally on track for a new life. But what makes you think she was involved in the accident?"

"When we were driving over to see the suite, she started telling me about her move and an accident with a deer crossing. A bell rang in my mind and I asked her about the date and bad weather. It's the same as Dave's."

Tom frowned. "That doesn't mean it was her car. That's a busy highway. However, Julie has been acting like a detective lately. She saw Tracey's SUV outside the café the other day and got the license plate number. She's convinced that Tracey was the driver that night."

Andre was quiet. "What should we do, Tom? I don't know what to think. The way she talked about it made me think that she didn't realize what happened. I believe what she said about the weather. I looked it up and there was a severe weather warning that night in that area. She didn't sound like she was lying about the crash, when she said she stopped at the next gas station to see what the damage was. I think she presumed Dave had gone by safely."

Tom sighed. "The reason she didn't see the other driver then was because he was already in the ditch. I can't imagine how frightening that must have been for Dave. We've talked with him since the accident. The RCMP apparently contacted him a week or two after it happened. He couldn't tell them anything about the crash because he was unconscious at the time. There was no one else at the scene to prove that it was Tracey who forced him off the road. I suppose we could get Dave's license plate number, if it's still in the scrap yard, which I doubt, and try to match them. Or just ask him if he remembers what it the number is. But Dave doesn't want to make a fuss over it. He says his leg is healing nicely now, and all he wants to do is get back to a normal life. He feels it's best just to leave things alone. I think we should too."

TWENTY-NINE

Tom was on his way home the afternoon that Dave and Ellie were expected to arrive in Rocky View. Peyton had called him earlier and invited him to come for dinner. He hadn't seen her since the wedding and was looking forward to it. It would be good to see them. He decided to go a bit early so he could bring a few things to help her with the preparations. Julie and Ed were coming and Jason too, with Herb and Anna. It would be a nice evening for them all.

When Tom arrived with some groceries, they smiled and hugged each other briefly. Peyton had been cooking and baking all day and the Lodge kitchen smelled delicious. Now she was setting the dining room table with the tablecloth and China that Julie had loaned for the showings. She was glad to see him and have his help. Minutes later, his phone beeped. "It's my friend Andre. He has wanted to see the renos for a long time and is wondering if he could come."

"What do you think, Peyton? Got room for one more?"

"Of course! The more the merrier! We have lots of food and a huge room to eat it in!"

"Actually, he wants to bring his girlfriend too."

"That's fine. We'll set up for two more."

Soon everything was completed and ready. Waiting

for Dave and Ellie to arrive, Tom and Peyton slipped out to the deck for a break. She wanted to tell him what had happened since they'd last met. She felt like he was the only person who would really understand. Tom was surprised about Dave's announcement that he was retiring. "Not only that, but Ellie is also retiring, and they're planning to get married. He says he wants to have a talk with me soon. Probably about our family home. I'm dreading the thought. I have so many precious memories of growing up there with Mom and Dad. I can't see myself living there with him and Ellie. Maybe they plan to live at her place. If he is, our home will have to be sold. I wouldn't be able to afford the upkeep."

"Honey, I'm sure Dave has a plan in mind. Why don't you just try to enjoy this evening? I'm sure things will work out for you. He loves you and wants you to be as happy as he is. Just give him a chance to explain everything to you."

When Dave and Ellie arrived, Peyton hugged her dad and started to cry. They had been apart for so long and she'd worried so much about him. To see him looking so healthy and happy was wonderful and made her tear up. Tom grabbed some tissues and held them out to her. She smiled at him gratefully and she could see the love in his eyes.

"How was the trip, Dave? It's a lovely day for it."

"It was great, Tom. I'd forgotten how beautiful this country is. I've spent so much time in and out of the hospital and physiotherapy clinics! It feels great to be able to travel again."

"Well, we're glad to see you looking so good. And you too Ellie." He teased her. "I hear you folks are going to be the first couple to stay in the renovated Lodge."

"As matter of fact we are, Tom. Yesterday Ellie and I went to Calgary City Hall and got married."

Peyton was shocked. "Dad, why didn't you tell me? We could have put on a big shindig for you!"

"Not necessary, sweetheart. We're just happy to be here with you. Being with family and friends is all we want. Looks like we're going to have a lovely dinner together, and staying in this beautiful Lodge can be our honeymoon!"

Ellie smiled. "We're celebrating our retirements too. We wanted you to be a part of that too."

"Well, that is something to celebrate. Congratulations to you both!"

The other guests were coming in and Tom was taking coats. When Andre and Tracey arrived, Tom was suddenly worried. Why had Andre brought Tracey? What if it was true that she was on the highway with Dave that terrible night? There was no proof, but Julie seemed to believe that it was Tracey's vehicle had caused the accident. She had seen Tracey in the café and spoken to her. What if Julie, Peyton and Tracey connected with each other tonight? What if Dave suddenly remembered the accident? Would there be trouble?

Tom took Andre aside. "Why did you bring Tracey tonight? Don't you realize what the consequences might be?"

"Yes, I thought about it. That's why I brought her. I think it would be good for Dave and Tracey to talk with each other about the accident. Maybe it wasn't Tracey that night. Then Julie and Peyton would be at rest. If it was her, she would be able to tell her side of the story. Dave has already said that he doesn't want any fuss. It's time for them both to face each other and get over it."

Tom studied Andre for a moment. "I think it's you that wants to get over it. Are you in love with Tracey, by any chance?"

Andre smiled. "Let's just say that I think she's beautiful

and smart and I want to know her better. And I want to see how she handles this situation. We may or may not have a future together."

After the dinner was over, Jason and his parents volunteered to do the cleanup, and Ellie and Julie went upstairs to prepare a room for the couple. Andre turned on the huge fireplace in the great room, and the folks took their drinks and sat around it. Dave and Ellie were pleased with the lovely dinner and the opportunity to stay at the Lodge. After a few minutes of chatting, Andre brought up the matter of Dave's accident without mentioning names or dates. At first, Tracey was only mildly interested but the more he told the story, the more excited she became. "You know, I had the same experience a while ago. On the highway, coming from Calgary. May 29th."

As the conversation continued, things began to dawn on everyone. "That evening I was driving in the rain, following a red Dodge pickup. A deer jumped in front of my car and I swerved into the pickup. I knew that I had bumped into it but it didn't seem that hard. I couldn't stop to see because it was so stormy. Tell me. Was that you?"

"If you own a black Subaru, it may have been. That was a scary night. We bumped against each other and I tried to stay on the road but my wheels got caught in the gravel. It pulled me right into the ditch."

Tracey's face was pale. "I was trying to pass, when I saw the deer in front of me. I was so startled that I swerved to the right and then a hard left and then I was heading toward the median. I tried to keep on the road and it was so slippery. I managed to get back but had no idea that you went into the ditch."

Peyton was disgusted. "It was you that caused my father's accident. Do you realize what you did to him? He ran into a deep ditch, hit a huge tree and smashed in the whole front of the truck. And you never even stopped to see what it was? He was unconscious for hours before anyone came! When someone finally noticed the lights on the truck, they called an ambulance, which didn't come for a long time. Turned out that his leg was broken in two places, and he had to have surgery with rods put in. He's been laid up for months. All because of you."

"I'm so sorry, Dave. I didn't stop because by the time I got back on my side and calmed down, I didn't realize that had happened, and I assumed that we both were okay. I stopped at the next service station, thinking you might be there, but you weren't."

Tracey was crying by this time and Andre had gone over to her chair and put an arm around her. Dave was calm. "From the sound of it, you're not to blame. It was an accident, on a slippery road in the dark, on a stormy night. These things happen. You did what you had to, to save your own life. You know, when I saw you come in tonight, I thought I had seen you before. We must have seen each other's faces, just in a flash, when you were passing me."

"I'm so sorry that did that. I'm used to travelling fast. If only I'd stayed behind you!"

"It was my fault too. I was driving way too slow. It had been a long day and my truck was loaded with equipment and tools. I was really tired and probably should have been paying more attention. Please don't think that it was your fault, my dear. It could have happened to anyone. The whole thing has turned out to be a blessing. If the accident hadn't happened, I wouldn't have met Ellie. She was the nurse that looked after me that night and during the weeks after. Now she's my beautiful wife. You know, folks, I believe the Lord was with us that rainy night. Things could have been more serious than they were, and much good has come from it. We must be grateful, not angry with one another."

THIRTY

Peyton called Julie and they arranged to meet at the café for lunch. She was excited to tell her aunt about her decision to stay in Rocky View. So much to think about! She could stay on the property until the lodge sold, but then she would have to find another place to park her motorhome. If that happened soon, perhaps Tom would let her park it on his property until she could rent a place in Rocky View. Then she had to go back to the city for the rest of her belongings. Their family home might be sold quickly in such a large city, so she wanted to be sure her things were cleared out. She wasn't sure how long Dave and Ellie were planning to stay at the Lodge. Maybe when they were ready to go back to the city, she would ask for a ride. She needed her own car, which was still in Calgary, and then she'd be able to start the ball rolling.

Helen was walking up the street when she noticed Peyton's motorhome drive up. They hadn't seen one another for a while. She waited until Peyton parked and then approached the door. Peyton was pleased to see her and they hugged each other tight. Peyton had loved this beautiful woman ever since they met at dinner in her lovely apartment. It seemed like it was a long time ago but it was only a few weeks.

"I missed you, Helen! Tom told me that you were

having a surgery and I've been meaning to get in touch. How are you doing? Feeling better?"

"Oh, I'm doing well. I had my surgery. There was a tumor but it was small and surrounded by healthy tissue so they were able to remove it. And apparently my liver function is good."

"That's wonderful, Helen. I'm so glad to hear that. I have some good news for you too. The Lodge project has been successfully completed and it's now up for sale. And I've decided that I love this town and all of you so much that I never want to leave. I'm going home to pack my things and then move back!"

"What? Really? That's wonderful, Peyton. Oh, I'm so happy! Does Tom know?"

"Not yet. But I came to town to tell him. I called him but it went to voicemail. Maybe he's busy at work."

"I don't think he would be there. I saw him earlier and he told me he had the day off."

Just then the café doorbell across the street jingled and they looked over. They were both dismayed to see Tom and Tracey come out and pause on the step to hug one another. Tom was smiling and she was gazing up at him. She put both hands on his face and pulled his head down, and it looked d like she kissed him!. It was only a moment but enough to horrify Peyton. She turned away and Helen stopped her. She was surprised but not as much as Peyton. "Tom and Tracey have known each other for years, honey, ever since high school. They were sweethearts for a while but Tom broke it off. He told me she wasn't his type and I thought so too. I wouldn't worry about this one. Tom is a gentleman and she probably just caught him off guard. You must know by now that Tom is in love with you."

"If he is so in love with me, why did he not notice

my motorhome? It's pretty hard not to. Maybe there's something going on between them. He didn't even look my way. Tracey looked so happy. I need to go, Helen."

She scrambled into the motorhome and started the engine but then realized that other vehicles had boxed her in, front and back. Lunch time was a busy time. Frustrated, she opened the door and stepped down… into the arms of Tom.

"You need to turn the engine off before you climb down. If you're thinking of lunch, the café is full. I think you'll have to wait until these folks finish their lunch and give up their space. You're taking up several spots as it is."

"Did you enjoy your lunch with your girlfriend? You seemed very satisfied when you came out of the café."

"What? Do you mean Tracey? She's not my girlfriend. And I haven't had my lunch yet. Mom and I are meeting for lunch."

"Helen and I were chatting and we saw you and Tracey come out. We saw you kiss her!"

"You mean, she kissed me, just a peck. That's her tendency when she's happy. She told me she had good news. She and Andre just got engaged. He's in the café, paying for their lunch and telling his friends that he's getting married."

Peyton was embarrassed but Helen chuckled and looped arms through both of theirs. "Let's go have lunch somewhere else. I'm famished! There's other good news you'll be happy to hear, my son. But let's celebrate it over my favorite Chinese food!"

Over lunch, Peyton broke the news that she was going to move to Rocky View. Tom's face lit up like the sun! Helen and Peyton smiled at his reaction. Helen made sure she took up one side of the table, and Peyton and Tom sat on the other, side by side. He had to be reminded that there was food getting cold on his plate. While they were eating, Helen silently rejoiced. Peyton had no doubts now about their relationship.

Helen had other news that she wanted to share, although she wasn't sure how Tom would like it. "I had a visit from your dad this week and we had a long conversation. He wants to connect with you again, Tom. He told me that all through the years he had been keeping track of you boys, although you never knew it. He kept at a distance for your sake as well as for his other family. But now he wants his daughter and sons to know you too."

"Mom. I don't think so. I really have no interest in what he or his family does. Allen feels the same way, I'm sure. Our father left us and that's the end of it. He got what he wanted back then and it's not fair of him to expect us to do anything else for him now."

"Tom, I was just as devastated as you, perhaps even more. When my husband left me with you two boys to raise on my own, my heart was broken! I was shocked and afraid that I wouldn't be able to carry on. If it wasn't for the good Lord, and the support of our church and community, I would have lost my mind. But we pulled through. And you, especially, were my rock in the hard times and still are. I'm so proud of you for that. Now my past love, who cheated on me for so many years and fathered three other children, is expecting me to welcome them all into our family. The very thought of it has been upsetting for me. But after thinking it over, I'm willing to give it a try. You have two half-brothers and a half-sister. You all deserve the opportunity to at least meet one another."

Tom sighed. "What do you want to do, Mom?"

"It's been done, Tom. I have invited Peter to bring his other family to dinner at your home, and I expect all of you to come - Allen, and Charlene and the baby too. I want you and Peyton to help me with the meal, and I will need to use your home and kitchen. I'd love to have it at my place but there wouldn't be enough room."

"Have you set a date, Mom?"

"Not yet. I want each of you to consider this and come to terms with the idea. I want it to be a peaceful evening without any bad feelings. Peter has agreed to contact his sons, who are studying at the university in Calgary, to see when they would be free to come, and his daughter has said that she would like to come. If you don't mind, I would appreciate you telling Allen about it for me. He was pretty upset the last time he met Peter. Maybe you can talk him into being a gentleman."

THIRTY-ONE

Dave and Ellie stayed at the lodge for a few more days, then announced that they were going back to the city. Both homes had been put up for sale and their realtors were already getting interested buyers. They needed to be there.

Peyton hitched a ride with them so she could go home and start packing. It was going to be a big job! Twenty years ago, Dave had built their house with help from family and friends, and although only three people had ever lived there, the contents were plenty. It would take quite a while to go through everything and decide what to sell or take with them. In case their family home sold quickly, she wanted to have things sorted.

Tom had offered to take a few days off to help them with the move but Peyton declined. "Thanks for offering, but I'd rather do it on my own. I'm not sure how long it will take for me to clear up things. I'll probably stay here until the house is actually sold and it's time to move out. If it takes too long, I'll just close up the house and hire a truck to bring my stuff to Rocky. I'll keep you posted."

Going through a house with so many memories and having to choose what to keep was hard for Peyton. She had to sort not only the household stuff, but the personal things - her own, her father's and her mother's. When

Melissa passed, neither of them could bear to dispose of any of her personal belongings, so her clothing was still in her dresser drawers and hanging alongside Dave's in their closet. Family pictures, knickknacks and books she had treasured for so long were still on the shelves. Seeing all that now brought tears to Peyton's eyes. Now that her dad was married, she wasn't quite sure what to do with it all. When she asked him about it, he said he would be living at his new bride's home until it was sold. "I will take the things I need and want to her place. I'd like you to go through the rest of the stuff here and keep anything you want. If you are in doubt about some things, just put them aside and we'll talk about them later. As far as the furniture goes, think about what you want to keep and we'll figure out how we can ship them. The rest you can sell or give to charity. I will be helping Ellie with her packing too, so I've ordered a whole bunch of boxes to be delivered to our house and to Ellie's. These are new chapters in our lives, sweetheart. I know this is hard for you but right now but wonderful things lie ahead for us both."

For the next few weeks, Dave spent time in both homes, which both women were thankful for. In the afternoons he could be heard clearing out his garage, which was a big job. Peyton continued to sort out the things in the house that she thought she should keep for herself and Dave. He seemed to be avoiding anything that reminded him of Melissa, and Peyton felt a bit hurt about it. But she remembered what their life was like when cancer was part of it, and Dave was so devastated. That was in the past and Peyton didn't want to stir anything up now, so she kept the memories of that part of their lives to herself.

Peyton was pleased when she got a call from Julie,

who had been busy with several other clients for the last couple of weeks and hadn't provided them with any news about the Lodge. She was excited now, calling to report that a substantial offer for the Lodge had just been made, for much more than any of them had expected. Julie wasn't going to say more until they were all together.

"That's great, Julie! Have you contacted Dad too?"

"Yes, I have. He wants us together online as soon as possible so we can discuss it."

"He's over at Ellie's house right now."

"No, he's not." The front door creaked open and Dave and Ellie came in smiling. "Hi, everyone! We brought donuts to celebrate."

They sat around the kitchen table and Julie turned her tablet so they all could see her. "I know you're anxious to know the amount offered. You've worked so hard and done such a wonderful renovation that you should be very proud of yourselves. You deserve every penny." She grinned and hesitated just for effect. "Remember when we were trying to figure out how much we wanted for the Lodge? Well, the buyers are offering that and more."

Peyton was stunned at Julie's words. "Really? That's amazing! Why would they offer more than we're asking for? Does that make sense? Who are these people?"

"You're looking at them."

"What? You're joking."

"Dave and Ellie. They are the buyers. They're offering one million dollars for the Lodge."

Peyton was speechless. She looked over at Dave for a response. "Honey, Ellie and I sold both of our homes this past week. We didn't want to tell you until we had everything figured out. Here it is. We want to buy the Lodge and make it our home and business for the rest of our lives. With the money we're getting from selling our own homes, we'll have enough to pay off the company bank loan and renovation costs and open the Lodge again."

"Wow! "This is wonderful, Dad! How long have you two been planning this?"

Ellie answered. "Ever since we came to see you at the site, I guess. When you showed us around the Lodge the first time, we really liked it and got the idea of buying a small hotel somewhere. It seemed like a good idea for our retirement years. Dave has been keeping in touch with Peyton from the beginning of the project and as the renovations continued, we got more and more interested. We began to think about marrying and retiring to this Lodge. That's why we wanted to see it a second time. We were absolutely convinced then. We love it and we know it will be a wonderful experience to own and operate it."

Peyton was delighted. "That's wonderful, folks! I'm so happy that we'll all be together in Rocky View."

Julie spoke up. "Congratulations, folks! I'll sign off now and get busy with the contract documents. If you have any questions, please feel free to call me."

Ellie and Peyton clapped hands in excitement, and Dave watched in pleasure. "There will be lots to do for the next few weeks, with all of us moving to the Rockies. And we'll have to get cracking if we want to have the Lodge ready for summer tourists. We'll need to furnish all the rooms and stock them with bedding, towels and basic toiletries and so much more!"

Dave and Ellie were ready to go home but he wanted a few words with Peyton. "Kitten, I've been thinking a lot about our business. I don't want to close it. Now that we're both moving to Rocky View, maybe we could keep Carmichael Construction going. I'm sure I'll be very busy helping my partner at the Lodge. But you could work once you get settled there. You're a carpenter and you could do small jobs, or help people remodel their homes or businesses. If you decide to continue with flips, I might even be able help you with that now and then, once my leg heals."

"What about our property here, Dad? Is it completely closed?"

"Not yet. I told them I was retiring but that hasn't happened yet. We could make this place the Calgary Carmichael Construction Main Office and open a satellite office in Rocky View. That way, we'd have two places to work from. This manager and his crew could continue the work we have been doing for so many years. They are people that we can trust. We would keep in touch."

"Good idea, Dad. Thanks for suggesting. I was a bit worried about finding work when I go back there, but if we keep the business operating, we could do other projects too. It's going to be great! I'm so glad things turned out this way, and we'll be living near each other!"

THIRTY-TWO

The next afternoon, Peyton was in the attic of her house, trying to wrestle boxes down to the second floor. The place was dusty and made her sneeze a lot. Rows of boxes were labelled Christmas ornaments, children's toys, old clothes and tax returns from years ago. Their artificial tree was shadowing the light and tangled with spider webs. She hated doing this but she couldn't ask Dave to help. He was still a bit wobbly with that leg. Even though the stuff was useless now, she didn't want to leave anything behind.

She heard the doorbell ringing and was struggling to get down when she knocked the ladder over on a lamp. It crashed down over the coffee table and she yelled in frustration. Now what! How was she going to get down? She would have to jump even though she was bound to get hurt. She took a deep breath and leaned forward.

"Stop! Don't jump!"

Peyton looked up in surprise. "Tom! Am I glad to see you!" He grabbed the ladder and helped her down, and they hugged each other. "Thank you for rescuing me. But what are you doing here?"

"I should ask you that question! Your dad contacted me and asked that I come to help you with your move. I told him I'd already offered and you refused, but he insisted. Why are you here alone, dragging stuff down from the attic? That's a dangerous thing to do."

"I know. But I need to get things done here. Dad sold the house this week and we need to pack everything up. The people who bought it have specified we only have 30 days to move out."

"Dave told me about the house sales and their purchase of the Lodge. That's wonderful and I'm really happy for them both. It's going to be nice having your family in Rocky View and I think they'll be terrific hotel owners. The whole town will be buzzing when the Lodge opens again. It will make a big difference in our economy."

"I'm so glad you're here, Tom. I've been doing this on my own for a few days and I didn't realize how hard it was going to be. Physically and emotionally. I didn't want Dad to work too hard so I coaxed him to do what he could in the garage. I said I would look after the house but the job is more difficult than I thought."

"Well, here I am. At your service. Let's finish the attic cleaning and then have some have some lunch. I'm starving!"

As they munched at a nearby cafe, Peyton asked Tom if he knew of any vacant apartments. "Dad doesn't want to keep much of our furniture because Ellie already has a houseful. I can take as much as I want but how much I keep depends on the size of the apartment I rent."

Tom looked at her and smiled. "What's all this about renting an apartment? If I have any say in it, let me tell you what I think. I know of a lovely log home, just around the curve from the Rocky View Lodge. It has had only one tenant for the last five years and he is very lonely, and so is his dog."

Peyton jaw dropped and she smiled. Her eyes moistened as he reached over and took her hand. "My sweet girl, this isn't the time or place that I'd planned to do this, but I'm going to do it anyway." He reached into his jacket pocket and pulled out a small box, then slid out of the booth and knelt on one knee. Peyton gasped.

"You can bring as much of your belongings to Rocky View as you please, because my house is huge and empty, and has been for years. I've been waiting for just the right person to share it with me. And now I've found her. Peyton Carmichael, will you marry me?"

Peyton clasped her hands and looked at him with tears in her eyes. "Oh, Tom!"

"Honey, I fell in love with you the first time we met. Over these last few months, as we got to know each other better and better, you've not only become my best friend but a part of my family. And my love for you has grown so strong that I know you're the only one I want to spend the rest of my life with. I love you so much, Peyton. Please say yes?"

Peyton smiled through her tears. "Yes! Oh, yes!"

Tom took her hand and lifted her out of the booth to embrace and kiss her. Nearby customers cheered and clapped. For a moment they were in another sphere as they kissed again and again. Then laughing, they gathered up their coats and left the cafe. They had something wonderful to tell their families. It would be a happy day for them all!

THIRTY-THREE

T hree weeks later, two moving vans pulled out of the city, on their way to Rocky View, one with Dave and Ellie's possessions, and the other with Peyton's. The three of them had gone ahead with their vehicles, travelling in convey. They remembered what happened to Dave and didn't want to take a chance of anything bad happening this time, so they agreed to keep together and stop for frequent breaks along the way. This would be the first time Dave had sat behind the wheel of a vehicle since his accident, and Peyton was a bit worried about him. But he assured her that he was doing well driving his new pickup, and proud of it.

All three vehicles were packed tight with things they were bringing from the city. Dave and Ellie in particular, were excited about stocking the Lodge and setting a date for the opening. Before they left the city, they had gone to several companies and bought products that were needed at the Lodge, purchasing as much as they could take in their vehicles this time, and setting up accounts so they could order more as needed. Larger amounts and items would be shipped to Rocky View in the next few days.

Peyton was missing Tom. She hadn't seen him for two weeks. Shortly after the day he proposed, he had gone back to Rocky View. She understood that he had to look after his business, but now that they were engaged, she longed to be with him, more and more. They had spoken every night by phone since then, but it wasn't enough. Now she was on the way to him and excited.

Her cell phone rang and it was Tom. "Hi, sweetheart! How are you? Did you have enough help to load?"

"Yes, we did fine. Dad rounded up some of his buddies and they helped us a lot. We left the city two hours ago. Both moving vans are on their way too. How are things at the log yard?"

"Slow today. I'm working in the office because my receptionist phoned in sick and my crews are taking a break. Two of them have completed our part of their homes and are now overseas with our logs. I thought of you and wanted to hear your voice."

Peyton smiled. "I miss you so much, Tom. Are you going to be there when we arrive tonight?"

"Absolutely! Give me a call when you get close. I've been sitting here thinking about something that I want to run by you. A date for our wedding day."

"I've been thinking about that too, Tom. If I had my way, we would just go to the courthouse and get married tomorrow. I don't want a big fancy wedding. But we do need a little time to arrange something. Our families expect that."

"Well then, let's do something like what Allen and Charlene did. In the church, simply dressed, not too many people, and a reception in the church basement."

"You're so well known and loved, Tom, that a lot of folks would want to attend. How about something simple but bigger, in the town square? We can rent a big tent and decorate it for the ceremony. Pastor Bob would officiate, I'm sure. For the reception, we'll get our church ladies to cater, bring in some professionals, or both. Let's do it! Alfresco! Let's hope the weatherman co-operates."

The drive to Rocky View was smooth and when the three vehicles reached there, they split off and went to the two locations, Ellie and Dave to the Lodge, and Peyton to Tom's home up the road from there. Tom had arranged for helpers to be at each place for the unloading of the two semi-trucks. Peyton was thankful that so many friends had come to help. Allen and other workers from the log yard were there, as well as Jason and his parents, who were happy to help. The boys from the church youth group came too, after school let out.

Dave and Ellie were moving into the Lodge, and their furniture and other belongings would be stored on the top floor where the master suite was. They were hoping that later in the year, they could build a small house behind the Lodge to live in, freeing up the master suite in the Lodge for guests.

Peyton directed the other semi to Tom's house to unload her furniture and other belongings from her family home. She would be staying at Helen's until after their wedding. She could stay in the motorhome, which was now parked in his yard, but it wouldn't be right. Small town gossip could be hurtful. She would not live with Tom in his home, or the motorhome, until after they married.

After unloading everything at both places, Tom invited everyone to come to his home for an awesome supper that Helen and Charlene had been working on all afternoon. Everyone was tired and the thought of a rest, and lovely meal, was too good to resist. The ladies had set up tables and chairs, enough for everyone, even the truck drivers. The aromas coming from the kitchen and backyard barbecue were mouthwatering and the buffet table looked luscious. "You've outdone yourselves, ladies. Thank you so much for this!"

"You're welcome, Dave. It's wonderful to be together with all of you. We're so happy that Peyton is going to stay here, and that you folks bought the Lodge." Helen helped Peyton put the dishes on the buffet table and turned to speak. "Tom, would you like to pray before things get cold?"

"My pleasure! Lord, I thank you for this day, and for the blessings it has brought to my home. Thank you for protecting those who travelled here to their new homes. I'm so grateful that they're now going to be part of our family. Thank you for those who made this lovely meal in celebration of what lies ahead. And most of all, thank you for bringing my beautiful fiancé into my life. She is the one that I was waiting for, all these years."

EPILOGUE

The grand re-opening of the Rocky View Lodge was a success! Furnishing such a large hotel was costly but well worth it. Both Peyton and Ellie had a knack for decorating and had a wonderful time making the Lodge beautiful. The ground floor woodwork and floors were cleaned and polished, and each one of the second-floor bedrooms were different but all were amazingly beautiful. Anna had been re-hired to her previous job as the front desk receptionist and assistant to Ellie, the Hotel Manager. They were also doing the advertising and connecting with customers from all over the country, and the world, who were interested in visiting the Rocky Mountains. Dave was the Hotel Maintenance Engineer and was enjoying working with Jason to keep things working well, inside and out.

Tom and Peyton were married in the town square, as they wanted to. So many people came that Helen worried there wouldn't be enough food to serve after the ceremony. But Helen and her pals had been hard at work for weeks prior to the Day and there was plenty for everyone, including potluck donations that kept coming well into the evening. Tom and some fellows from the Log yard had built a large dance floor and set up some music for the event, so Tom and Peyton could have their first dance together. They noticed later in the evening that Andre and Tracey were dancing close together and wondered if wedding bells would soon be ringing for them!

Peter and his sons and daughter had been invited to the wedding and were enjoying the event. Weeks ago, they had come together at the dinner Helen had held for them and it was surprisingly nice. Once they introduced themselves to one another, there was no talk about the past and everyone was polite and courteous with each other. When Peter said they lived in Jasper, everyone was interested in talking about the place, so it broke the ice for Tom and Allen, who were both excellent skiers who had spent many winter events there. Dave and Peyton had been there years ago when Melissa was alive, but Ellie was born and raised in Ontario and had never been to the Rockies. Helen was pleased how well the dinner went. The young people seemed to be connecting with one another and she hoped that it would continue.

After the evening died down and most of the folks had left the square, Peyton and Tom sat down with Allen and Charlene to relax. The evening stars were beautiful something that Peyton rarely saw because of all the lights in the city. Baby Jasmine was asleep in Tom's arms. He loved being her uncle and cherished the thought of he and Peyton having children of their own.

"We have some news for you, now that everyone has gone home." Allen and Charlene were smiling. "Jasmine wanted a brother. So...I'm pregnant!"

"What? That's great!" Tom was so happy that he woke up the baby. "We thought you were looking a little plumper lately. Just kidding!"

"How do you know it's a boy?" Peyton wasn't familiar with this.

"I had an ultra-sound and we could tell from that."

"I'm so happy for you guys. When do you expect his birth?"

"I'm three months now, so probably around Christmas time."

"Nice time to present the little fellow to the family. Congratulations to you both!"

When Allen and Charlene left for home, Tom turned the music back on low and took Peyton into his arms. "Finally, we're alone! It's been quite a day, hasn't it? Are you happy, Peyton?"

"I couldn't be any more, my love!" She took his head in her hands and kissed him. His response was long and breathless. They danced for a few more moments in the warm evening light. "I'm the happiest man in the whole wide world tonight. Remember that song about the keeper of the stars? That's how I feel tonight. I waited so long for the person that God wanted me to have as my bride. And now you are mine. I'm so thankful that you came into my life. I want us to be together for all our lives and have a family that we love and treasure. Let's go home."

ABOUT THE AUTHOR

I have been an avid reader ever since I was a child, and as I grew older it was all about princes, princesses, and castles, and later on, mysteries. I was a great fan of Nancy Drew! I wanted to write a book like her and I wrote my first one in Grade Five. I showed it to my friends and they loved it. My teacher praised me but took it away so I could continue my schoolwork. When I got into my teens, my mother introduced me to books she owned, ones she loved as a Christian woman. She made sure there was beauty in the stories, and I have followed in her steps.

As an adult I wrote many things over the years. Most of my writing consisted of my work as a social worker, pastor, and community services worker in various areas of the country. I tried to write my book in my spare time, but it never got very far. When I retired and was diagnosed with Alzheimer's Disease, I resolved to finish the book before I was unable to do it anymore. With God's help, it has finally been possible!

Printed in the United States
by Baker & Taylor Publisher Services